Books by Sarah Crossan

The Weight of Water
Apple and Rain

apple

AND

RAIN

SARAH CROSSAN

BLOOMSBURY

NEW YORK   LONDON   OXFORD   NEW DELHI   SYDNEY

First published in Great Britain in August 2014 by Bloomsbury Publishing Plc
Published in the United States of America in May 2015 by Bloomsbury Children's Books
Paperback edition published in October 2016
www.bloomsbury.com

Bloomsbury is a registered trademark of Bloomsbury Publishing Plc

For information about permission to reproduce selections from this book, write to
Permissions, Bloomsbury Children's Books, 1385 Broadway, New York, New York 10018
Bloomsbury books may be purchased for business or promotional use. For information on
bulk purchases please contact Macmillan Corporate and Premium Sales Department at
specialmarkets@macmillan.com

Extracts taken from *Opened Ground* © Estate of Seamus Heaney and reprinted by
permission of Faber and Faber Ltd

The publishers are grateful for permission to adapt "Stevie Scared" from *The House
That Caught a Cold*, first published by Puffin Books, © Richard Edwards 1991

The Library of Congress has cataloged the hardcover edition as follows:
Crossan, Sarah.
Apple and Rain / by Sarah Crossan.
pages   cm
Summary: When her imagined perfect life with her estranged mother begins to unravel,
fourteen-year-old Apple finds comfort in reading and writing poetry.
ISBN 978-1-61963-690-3 (hardcover) • ISBN 978-1-61963-691-0 (e-book)
[1. Mothers and daughters—Fiction. 2. Sisters—Fiction.
3. Family problems—Fiction. 4. Poetry—Fiction.] I. Title.
PZ7.C88277Ap 2015   [Fic]—dc23   2014033266

ISBN 978-1-68119-073-0 (paperback)

Typeset by Hewer Text UK Ltd., Edinburgh
Printed and bound in the U.S.A. by Berryville Graphics Inc., Berryville, Virginia
2 4 6 8 10 9 7 5 3 1

All papers used by Bloomsbury Publishing, Inc., are natural, recyclable products
made from wood grown in well-managed forests. The manufacturing processes
conform to the environmental regulations of the country of origin.

For my grandmothers, Olive Fox and Mamie Crossan,
and for Andreas and Aoife, of course

PART 1
solitude

I don't know if what I remember is what happened or just how I imagine it happened now I'm old enough to tell stories. I've read about this thing called childhood amnesia. It means we can't remember anything from when we were really small because before three years old we haven't practiced the skill of remembering enough to be able to do it very well. That's the theory, but I'm not convinced. I have one memory from that time. It never changes, and if I wanted to make up memories, wouldn't they be good ones? Wouldn't all my childhood stories have happy endings?

*   *   *

I woke up crying. I could hear angry voices downstairs and thunder outside. I got up and stumbled onto the landing. A white gate was attached to the newel post to

3

stop me tumbling down the stairs. I couldn't figure out how to open it, no matter how hard I tried. I wasn't wearing socks. My feet were cold. I carried a white blanket that dragged across the floor.

Two figures stood by the front door under a sprig of mistletoe, their faces in shadow. I whimpered. Nana looked up. "Back to bed, pet," she said. "Go on now."

"Can't sleep," I said.

Nana nodded. "I know. I could never sleep before Christmas Day either."

I shook my head. It was nothing to do with Christmas. I just didn't want to go back to bed. The thunder sounded like it might blast through my bedroom window. And why was everyone shouting?

I started to cry again. I wanted the person in the green coat next to Nana to turn around because, although I could tell from her long hair and narrow waist she was a woman, I couldn't see her face.

But she wouldn't look up. She was staring at the doormat and holding tight to the handle of a suitcase.

"I'll call you in a few days," a voice from inside the green coat whispered, and I knew then it was my mum.

"Mummy," I said.

She opened the front door with her free hand. When

Nana tried to stop her stepping into the night, she shrieked and pushed my grandmother against the mirror on the wall. "Stop trying to ruin my life!" my mum shouted. The wind slammed open the door. Rain came thrashing into the hall. The air smelled especially salty.

Finally Mum turned and saw me, but she didn't smile or wave or blow me a kiss. She stared like I was something strange and sad that she couldn't decipher.

Then she sniffed, turned, and left, banging the door behind her.

And it was quiet again.

No shouting.

And no thunder either.

"Mummy," I whispered.

"Mummy's gone, pet," Nana said. She climbed the stairs, opened the gate at the top, and lifted me into her arms. She was shaking. Her eyes were wet. "It's you and me now. You and me, okay?"

"Mummy," I repeated.

"Let's go to bed," Nana said. "And in the morning we'll see what Santa brought you."

But I didn't care about Santa's presents. All I could think about was what had been taken away.

Again and again I've asked Nana about the Christmas Eve that Mum left. I want to understand why she walked out. But when Nana tells me what happened, she makes it all Mum's fault. Mum was the one who ran off to New York to be on Broadway, without once thinking about the child she'd left behind. And every year when Christmas rolls around, it's the memory of that night—Mum in her green coat and the thunder crashing around the house—that consumes me.

"I'm not waiting a minute longer!" Nana calls.

"Another thirty seconds!" I shout. I pull my purple hoodie over my head.

"I'm counting to ten!" Nana replies.

I tumble out of my room and down the stairs. Nana is brushing her black coat free of Derry's hairs. I take my scarf from the hall stand and wrap it around my neck a few times.

Nana's been spending the morning peeling parsnips and potatoes for dinner. The brussels sprouts are soaking in broth, and the turkey is slow cooking in the oven. The whole house smells of orange and cranberry stuffing.

Unlike me, Nana still loves Christmas. Every year she plays her favorite carols on repeat and turns the volume up really loud when "In the Bleak Midwinter" comes on. The sound of her singing fills the whole house and forces me to hide out with Derry, our Labrador, in my room. Nana isn't really much of a singer, but she's very enthusiastic.

Nana leaves the clothes brush on the hall table and tucks her feet into a pair of navy, low-heeled slip-ons. "Where do you think you're going in those?" she says. She points at my sneakers. I don't answer because it's a rhetorical question. She uses them when she's annoyed. "We're going to Mass and it's *Christmas*."

"They're comfortable. And they're only a bit scuffed," I say.

Derry sniffs my feet, giving away the fact that they probably smell. I shoo him away with the toe of one sneaker.

"I don't mind what you wear as long as it's clean, and those old things are *not* clean. Wear some nice shoes, please," she says in her soft Irish voice that's both gentle and firm.

The only *nice* shoes I have are heavy and blister my heels. I'm about to tell Nana this, when her eyes meet a spot on my hoodie.

"Now come on, Apple, what are you playing at? You don't have a clean top on either?" she asks. I scratch at the spot where I dripped egg yolk this morning. I'd forgotten about it, and you'd think by Nana's tone and big bulging eyes that the blotch was poisonous. "It's my favorite top," I say. And I want to wear it. I want to wear it with my smelly sneakers.

"Get yourself up those stairs immediately and change, young lady," Nana says. She pinches her mouth into a prune. When she does this, there's no arguing. When she does this, I always wish my mum were still here.

In my room, I squeeze into a dress and a pair of too-tight lace-up shoes. The last time I wore this outfit was six months ago to Nana's friend's funeral. Since then, Nana hasn't stopped talking about death. She says things like, *Oh, you'll miss me when I'm six feet under like poor Marjorie* or *I don't want everyone wearing black to my*

8

funeral, Apple. A bit of pink here and there won't harm.
It's not good for a fourteen-year-old to be around someone who thinks she's going to drop dead any second. I
told Nana as much, and she laughed, flipping her head
back and showing off her black fillings and missing teeth.
But I didn't understand what was so funny.

When I get back downstairs, Nana is penning Derry
into the kitchen. His golden hair is all over her coat
again. "Much better," Nana says, seeing me. I go to
Derry and kiss his silky ears. He turns and slobbers all
over my mouth. Nana grimaces. "Oh, Apple, he licks
his boy bits and then you let him lick your face. It's disgusting."

Nana double-locks the front door and hurries ahead
of me down the path to the car. Seagulls squawk and
circle in the sky. A fog is climbing up the hill from the
beach.

I slip into the backseat, because Nana still won't let me
ride with her in the front, and do up my belt. My feet
already feel cut up from the shoes. I can hardly breathe in
the dress.

"Do you think she might come home today?" I ask.

"Who?" Nana says. I don't reply. She studies me in the
rearview mirror. "I don't think so, Apple. Do you?"

I shake my head. I know Mum isn't going to magically show up today or any other day. Just because she left at Christmas doesn't mean that's when she'll come back.

And who knows, she might never come back at all.

3

After dinner, Dad and Trish arrive from London carrying a bag of presents and a fancy trifle. Trish nips my cheek between her fingers, and Dad kisses the top of my head.

"Everything well with you?" he asks.

I nod.

"School ticking along?"

"Yeah."

"Sorry I missed the end-of-term concert."

"That's okay," I say.

"You'll have to play me a tune from it later," he says.

"Okay."

Even though Dad lives less than two hours away, I don't see him much. Not since Trish showed up.

Dad and Trish got married three years ago. It was completely out of the blue. One day he made me speak to Trish on the phone, and the next they asked me to be their bridesmaid. I said yes, not knowing I was going to be forced to wear a bright-yellow dress that made me look like a stuffed lemon. Trish only spoke to me once the whole day, to tell me to "cheer up" because she didn't want me spoiling the photographs. She really shouldn't have said anything because then I went out of my way to ruin them. I stuck out my tongue and rolled my eyes back in my head and even pretended to be crying. I thought it was hilarious until the photos got delivered and Dad went ballistic. He said he'd spent over a thousand pounds on the photographer and made me write a long, fake letter of apology to Trish.

She still hasn't forgiven me.

*   *   *

Nana tips custard all over the steaming Christmas pudding she's saved for Trish and Dad's arrival and serves everyone a dollop in a reindeer-patterned bowl. "We can have the trifle for supper," she says. "So, tell me now, how's the new house?"

"It's absolutely marvelous, isn't it, Chris?" Trish says. She touches Dad's arm.

"It's a lot of work keeping up a garden, but we were sick of being stuck in that flat," Dad says.

Nana wipes her hands on her apron and sits down. "Oh, I wouldn't give up my garden for anything. We have our own little herb patch now, don't we, Apple?"

I pop a piece of pudding into my mouth. "Um-hmm," I say. It's still scorching. I have to spit it back into the bowl to stop the skin peeling away from my gums.

Trish clears her throat.

Dad frowns. "I've warned you about your manners," he says.

When? Six months ago when you last bothered visiting? I want to snap back. But I don't.

"It was boiling," I say. I put down my spoon. "Sorry."

"So, Apple, I hear you're about to take your Grade Four in clarinet. That's brilliant." Trish smiles, keeping her thin red lips pressed together.

I shrug. "Yeah, but I don't enjoy playing it that much."

"But it's a wonderful accomplishment to be able to play an instrument," Nana says.

"I paid three hundred pounds for that clarinet, not to mention the cost of the lessons," Dad says.

"*Three hundred pounds*? That's more than our new coffee table cost," Trish announces.

I ignore her. "I didn't say I was giving up. I just don't *love* playing, that's all." But what I do love about the

13

clarinet is going to orchestra where I get to see Egan Winters.

Egan Winters can play the flute while kicking a football between his feet. He actually seems more like a drummer or a bass guitarist; he wears leather bracelets and ripped jeans and is without doubt the best-looking person in our whole school. Plus, he's a senior, which means he isn't immature like the boys in my class. I know he doesn't see me. I know I'm only "that eighth-grade girl with the clarinet" to him, if anything. But I can't stop my heart thumping every time I'm near him.

"Teenagers are so bad at sticking with things. It's because of all these new phones and apps and things," Trish says, as though she hasn't heard me telling everyone that I am *not* giving up the clarinet. She tucks her wispy blond hair behind her ears and daintily wipes her mouth with one of Nana's linen napkins. "How much are these smarty-pants phones anyway?" It isn't a real question; she's just trying to make Dad see how much I'm costing them. She's trying to say, *Your kid is far too expensive.*

I push away my pudding. I really don't feel like eating anything more. I hate Christmas. And I hate Trish. "I don't feel well. Can I be excused?"

Dad sighs. "You look fine to me," he says. He's trying

to act serious, but he's wearing a gold paper hat from one of the crackers and I can't help smirking. "Apollinia, it's important you learn to persevere with things. You can't be someone who gives up as soon as you get bored or the going gets tough. You don't want to be one of those people, do you?" His voice has gone all tight, and I wonder whether he's thinking about Mum: how she split up with him when she found out they were going to have a baby; how she ran away when she realized you couldn't stuff a baby into your handbag like a Chihuahua.

Dad's worst nightmare must be that I turn out like my mum.

Nana stands up and pours Dad some more red wine. "Why don't we open our presents now and talk about this another time?" She doesn't like arguments at Christmas. She's into peace and joy.

Dad is staring at me. He isn't speaking. He seems mesmerized by something in my face.

"Chris?" Trish says. She taps him and he flinches.

"We will continue this discussion," he says to me.

"Presents!" Nana says, and we follow her to the plastic tree in the sitting room where a few small, sad boxes sit waiting to be unwrapped.

*   *   *

I get a new pencil case and a book token from Nana, and an Argos gift card from Dad and Trish. I don't know what I'm supposed to get in Argos, but I say thank you, then sit in front of the TV with my legs draped over Derry, waiting for Christmas to be over.

EastEnders is on, and when Nana notices, she quickly changes the channel. "Don't you watch soaps, Bernie?" Trish asks. Nana's name is Bernadette. Trish is the only person I know who calls Nana "Bernie."

Nana points at me. "Not appropriate," she says.

"I'm not a baby," I say.

"You're not an adult either. When you are, watch what you like," Nana says.

Trish pretends to bite down on the tip of her thumb. "Oops. Hope I haven't opened a can of worms," she says. If I had the courage, I'd slap her right across the face.

"*Chitty Chitty Bang Bang* is on," Nana says. She forages for the remote control.

Trish helps her search and then draws in her breath gently. "Oh, I almost forgot. Here's another gift," she says. She hands me a package. Dad starts to chew the inside of his cheeks.

I peel back the tape. It's a white T-shirt. "Thanks," I mutter, without taking off all the paper.

"You didn't unwrap it properly," Nana says.

"You didn't *read* it," Trish says.

I shake open the T-shirt. Written in swirly letters are the words BIG SIS. I turn to Dad, who is pink around the jaw. Nana is staring at Trish with her mouth open.

"You're having a *baby*?" I say.

"What lovely news," Nana says. She rushes at Dad and kisses him like he's her own son, which is what people always assume when they see them together. But he isn't. Dad was simply unlucky enough to be dating my mum when she got pregnant, and Nana always felt sorry for him, like he wasn't as much to blame for a baby coming along as Mum was. So Mum couldn't go to university, but Dad took a train to Liverpool a month before I was born and spent the next three years studying economics and getting drunk. Mum was stuck in Brampton-on-Sea, and by the time Dad came back from university, she was gone. She'd had enough of changing diapers and waiting for Dad's help.

And she'd had enough of me too, I think.

I fold the T-shirt and tuck it under Derry's paws.

"We found out a few weeks ago," Trish says. Her face is full of pride.

Dad looks a bit sad.

"You must be delighted," Nana says. She is smiling so much it must hurt.

"We're thrilled," Trish says. She kisses Dad hard on the lips right in front of Nana and me. A bit of custard-flavored sick rises in my throat.

Nana laughs nervously. "I'm going to have to get out my knitting patterns," she says.

"Wait until we know what we're having, Bernie. I hate to see a baby in yellow," Trish says, even though she made her bridesmaids wear yellow all day for her stupid wedding.

I hold Derry's collar and lead him out of the room. "I think he needs to pee," I say, but no one is listening.

*   *   *

After Derry's done his business, I let him into the kitchen and close the door. I sit on the back steps. The ground is icy. The air is thick and hazy with frozen fog.

"You'll get piles," a stranger's voice says. I look up but it's too dark to see anything. I stand, afraid of who's watching, and see a boy by my back fence. "Hemorrhoids are nasty things. Can't say I even know what they are though."

"Why are you in my garden?" I ask.

"Because I'm talking to you," he says. "There's a big gap in this fence. Someone should repair it."

"I know there is, but until now no one decided to use it as a gate." I came outside to be alone. I'm not in the mood for people. "You're trespassing," I tell him.

"You're right. Someone call the police!" he shouts.

He steps over Nana's flower beds and stomps up our garden. He's wearing a sweater with a giant frog on it and a pair of green rubber boots that are far too big for him. His cheeks and forehead are smeared with what looks like black war paint.

"Are you going into combat?" I ask.

"Sort of. Dad forgot to go shopping. I reckon we'll be having pasta and rice pudding for Christmas dinner. Mum's furious, so I'm hunkering down outside until it blows over."

I noticed a new family move into the house behind ours a few weeks ago. It had been empty for so long, I thought it would stay that way—become a home for spiders, mice, and homeless people.

"I think your house is haunted," I tell him. I'm being mean, but I'm not really sure why.

"Yep. It's totally haunted. I hear ghoulish whispers at

night. I'm not worried though; it'll keep the robbers away."

I gaze at the moon.

"So why are you out here? Shouldn't you be working your way through a box of After Eights?" he says.

"Not that it's any of your business, but my dad and stepmum just told me they're having a baby, and my nan is trying to make me act like I'm pleased. So if you could leave me alone to be depressed, I'd appreciate it."

"Ugh. Babies are so boring. I don't know why everyone gets all freaky around them."

I shrug and look through the kitchen window into the sitting room where Trish is laughing and clapping. "I'd better go inside," I say.

"Okay," he says. He walks away. "What's your name?"

"Apple," I say hesitantly.

"Apple? Like Apple Blossom?"

I blink. Normally when I tell kids my name, they make a nasty joke about Crab Apples or Bad Apples or go on and on about iPads.

Not that Apple is even my real name. My given name is Apollinia Apostolopoulou, which hardly anyone is able to pronounce. So instead of even trying to get people to say it, I tell them my name is Apple. The Apostolopoulou bit is still there; I can't do anything about that, and I often wonder why Mum even gave me Dad's surname. She wasn't going out with him when I was born. And I don't think she loved him. But she went ahead and chose a Greek first name too. There must have been a reason. When she returns, I'm going to ask her all about it.

I wish she were here now. I wish she'd never left me in the first place.

"My real name is Apollinia," I tell him. "But people have been calling me Apple since I was a baby."

"Cool. All right. Well, nice to meet you, Apple. I'm Del." He hops over Nana's gnome. Its fishing rod is broken. "Oh, and happy Christmas." He vanishes through the gap in the fence.

"Happy Christmas," I say quietly, even though it's anything but happy.

The back door opens. "What are you doing out here?" Nana asks.

"Nothing."

"Do you want to catch your death? Come inside."

"I don't mind catching my death," I say.

Nana tuts. "Don't talk nonsense."

I pick at my nails. "Nana, did Mum send a message? Did she e-mail you?"

"Wouldn't I have told you? No, she didn't. I haven't heard from her in about a year, Apple. You know that."

"How hard is it to send a card?" I say. At least she could pretend to remember us. Give us a bit of hope.

"Stop worrying about that. It's Christmas. And you've had some lovely news. A little brother or sister, Apple, like you always wanted. Now let's go inside and crack open that tin of Quality Street chocolates."

"You bought Quality Street?"

"Of course I did," she says. I think for a minute she might hug me, but she doesn't. She nods briskly and pulls me inside.

"That's a good girl," she says. "Now close the door behind you. It's bitter out."

4

In English, our first lesson after the holidays, I sit next to Pilar and tell her Dad and Trish's news.

"But babies are so *cute*," Pilar says.

"They might be cute, but they're a lot of work. I hardly see Dad as it is."

Pilar glances at her wrist. "Ms. Savage isn't usually late. Do you think she's sick? She was coughing a lot last term."

"She smokes, that's why she was coughing." I say. "Did you get a new watch?"

"I got it for Christmas. The hands are made of real gold. What did you get?"

"Argos vouchers."

"Seriously? What are you going to buy with *those*?"

"An electric toothbrush." I've already looked online. It's the only thing that interests me. "Apparently it only takes one minute to brush, which will save me three minutes every single time and six minutes a day. Within a year I'll have saved thirty-six and a half hours."

Pilar looks unimpressed. "If you have any money left over you could get a bedside cabinet." She laughs, and then so do I, and we keep laughing and making jokes about what we could buy from Argos, until a tall man with sideburns and wearing a silky green scarf sweeps into the room. The class goes quiet. The man plops a pile of papers on Ms. Savage's desk.

"Good morning, eighth grade. I'm Mr. Gaydon," the man says.

Some boys at the desk next to mine titter, presumably because of the "gay" bit in his name, but no one else laughs. We're waiting to hear the news. Did Ms. Savage leave? Is she dead? No one liked her all that much. But at least we knew her.

"Your teacher has broken her leg in a skiing accident, so I'm afraid she won't be at school for several months." A few students mutter. Someone cheers. Mr. Gaydon acts as though he can't hear any of it. "I'm taking over. But don't worry, I won't ask you to go around the room telling me your names and something interesting about yourselves. To be honest, I hate icebreakers. They're always a bit embarrassing. Let's hope you all participate enough that I learn your names naturally. But if I learn your name *too* quickly, it's probably a bad thing." His voice is soft and confident and completely unlike Ms. Savage's, who sounds like she expects an argument to come of everything. He sits on the side of his desk. "I heard from the head of the department that you're starting a poetry unit this term." There are grumbles. Mr. Gaydon holds up his hands. "I was guilty of hating poetry when I was younger, but that's because I didn't know what it could do. Do any of you know what poetry can do?" he asks.

We all gape at Mr. Gaydon. Has the lesson begun? Are we being quizzed? After a short, awkward silence, Jim Joyce raises his hand. Mr. Gaydon nods, inviting him to speak. He doesn't know that Jim Joyce is a troublemaker.

Jim smirks. "Can poetry make a great lasagna?"

If Ms. Savage were here, he would be sent into the corridor for a comment like that. Mr. Gaydon just laughs. "What's your name?"

"Jim," he says.

"Well, I won't forget your name, Jim, that's the bad news. The other bad news is that your answer is way off the mark. But I think you knew that."

Jim gives Mr. Gaydon two thumbs up. "What about skateboarding? Can poetry skateboard?" he asks.

Mr. Gaydon shakes his head. "Oddly, no. And I reckon you've had enough guesses," he says.

Jim sits back and puts his hands behind his head.

Mr. Gaydon hops off his desk. "I'll tell you what I think it can do, but maybe in a few weeks you'll have an even better answer than mine. Poetry can teach us about ourselves. It can comfort us when we are in despair. It can bring joy. But not only that . . ." He lowers his voice. "It can open us up. It can make our worlds bigger and brighter and clearer. It can *transform* us."

"What did he say about *Transformers*?" Jim calls out. "Those films are *lame*."

Half the class sniggers. I don't think Jim's funny. Mr. Gaydon's trying to get us excited about something and all Jim can do is fool around. If I weren't such a coward, I'd tell him to shut up and listen for a minute.

"Right, settle down. Today we're going to read a poem by someone very famous and very dead called Alexander Pope." Mr. Gaydon reaches for a handful of papers. "It's called 'Ode on Solitude.' Can anyone tell me what solitude means?"

Donna Taylor raises her hand and the rest of us relax,

safe from being picked to speak for a while. Even though Donna's really smart, she's still the most popular girl in our year. It's probably because she wears a ton of makeup so she seems older than the rest of us. And she walks wiggly, like she's got salsa music playing in her head.

It's funny because at primary school Donna was shy. She hid under triangular, toadstool hair. She didn't have many friends. But at Artona Academy no one knew what she'd been, and she became something else. She transformed, and she didn't use poetry to do it. She just went to Boots.

"Solitude means being alone, sir," Donna says.

"Exactly. Good," Mr. Gaydon says. "Now this guy Alexander Pope had a few things to say about solitude." He quickly hands each of us a copy of the poem and perches on the edge of his desk again. He flourishes his own paper and says, "Listen to this: 'Happy the man, whose wish and care; A few paternal acres bound; Content to breathe his native air; In his own ground.'" Mr. Gaydon looks up from the poem for a second. He seems pleased with what he's just read.

"Sir, I don't understand Shakespearey stuff," Jim says.

Mr. Gaydon nods. "It isn't Shakespeare, Jim, but I hear

you. All the poet is really saying is that a person can be happy if he just enjoys being at home chilling out. Now, does anyone want to read the rest aloud for us?" Mr. Gaydon asks.

Donna's hand is up again and then she's reading. I try to block out her voice and imagine my own voice reading the poem. When we get to the last stanza, I mouth the words:

"*Thus let me live, unseen, unknown;*
Thus unlamented let me die;
Steal from the world, and not a stone
Tell where I lie."

Donna stops reading. We wait for Mr. Gaydon to write up a list of the difficult words from the poem on the board. Or to tell us to copy down a question into our exercise books. Instead, he closes his eyes. When he finally opens them, he dips his head like someone's said something really interesting.

"Sir, are you on drugs or something?" Jim Joyce asks.

We laugh nervously. This is cheeky, even for him.

Mr. Gaydon points at Jim. "Tell me, Jim, what did that poem say to you?"

We all watch, waiting for Jim to say something like, *It*

told me I had superpowers, or *It told me it was break-time*, but he stares blankly at Mr. Gaydon.

"Anyone else want to talk to me about the poem? Does the narrator see solitude as a bad thing?" He waits for some hands to go up, but none do. "Right, forget the poem. I know it's hard to understand on a first read-through. So how about you? Do *you* see solitude as a bad thing?"

I want to put up my hand and tell Mr. Gaydon what I know about solitude—that it isn't possible to be alone and happy. If it were, all the kids at school with no friends would go around beaming. Which they don't. They're miserable. They hide in the toilets at lunch or sit in the corner of the cafeteria, looking like there's a rain cloud about to burst above them. And when I'm alone, especially at night, I think of my mum all the way across the Atlantic in America, and I wish she were closer. I don't want to be without her all the time.

Mr. Gaydon scratches his sideburns. "You're all very quiet, but I suppose you must be a little rusty from the holidays, so I'll tell you what I think: the poet admires people who live and even die without needing the recognition of others. But the problem is, most of us do need people. Goodness, if I died and no one cared, I'd hate it.

What a curse we live with—needing others is sort of rub-bish, isn't it?"

He pauses again, and after a few moments, Iona Churchill raises her hand. "I would *hate* being alone all the time. I like talking to people," she says. "That's why I have this." She holds up her phone, a pink thing rimmed in silver rhinestones.

"Good point!" Mr. Gaydon says. "Phone companies make a lot of money from the fact that we like to com-municate with one another as often and as quickly as possible."

"I'd like people to leave me alone when I'm playing *Grand Theft Auto*," Michael Evans says. "And by people, I mean my mum."

Mr. Gaydon smiles. The discussion continues. Everyone is suddenly eager to contribute. It's not like any other English class I've been in. Usually we are given comprehension questions and are told to answer them "in full sentences" using "good spelling and clear hand-writing." Mr. Gaydon hasn't even asked us to pick up our pens.

By the end of the lesson, everyone is arguing about the pluses and minuses of solitude, and Mr. Gaydon is smil-ing. He turns to the board to write up some homework, and we protest—dutifully. "In one hundred words exactly, explain your views on the idea of solitude," Mr. Gaydon says, reading aloud what he's written. "It can be in prose, which is a normal paragraph, or if you're feeling ambitious, you could write a poem. I'm asking for one hundred words exactly because I want you to think carefully about the language you use. Keep it lean. Okay, have a good day, folks."

The bell sounds for the end of class, and we pack up.

On her way out, Donna Taylor stops at our desk. "Nice watch," she says to Pilar.

"Thanks!" Pilar says. She grins. "The hands are made of real gold."

"Cool," Donna says. She keeps walking, her hips swimming from side to side.

"Looks like you've got a new best friend," I tell Pilar.

"Yeah, right," Pilar says. She links my arm, and we rush off to PE.

* * *

Pilar and I are in the science lab waiting for Ms. Whyte to photocopy a work sheet. While I wait, I watch Nana push through the crowded playground and sit on one of the graffiti-covered benches. Her giant green umbrella is keeping the rain at bay. She is sucking on the straw of a juice box.

I sigh.

"What?" Pilar asks, her nose pressed against a tank of tadpoles and gunk.

"Nana's outside."

Pilar comes to the window. "You've got to tell her. No one else in eighth grade gets picked up anymore."

"I tried."

"Well, try harder. It's embarrassing, Apple."

"Here you go," Ms. Whyte says, scurrying into the classroom. She's carrying a box of folders and holding the biology work sheet between her teeth.

"Thanks, miss," I say.

Pilar and I are still packing up when Donna Taylor rushes into the room. "Miss, miss, I dropped my work sheet in a puddle," she says. She holds up a soggy piece of paper.

"Wait here." Ms. Whyte sighs and trudges off to use the photocopier again.

Donna smiles. "Are you in detention or something?"

"No. No, I needed a work sheet too," I say.

"And I'm waiting with Apple," Pilar adds. As though that isn't obvious.

Donna puts her hands behind her back. None of us say anything for about a minute. Then suddenly my stomach growls loudly.

"Was that *you*?" Donna asks.

I nod. My face flushes—I don't exactly have the figure of someone who starves herself.

"I'm going down to the pier for french fries with Hazel and Mariah in a minute. If you two want to come, you can," Donna says. She doesn't seem very enthusiastic, but I'm not sure that matters. The point is that Donna Taylor has asked *us* to hang out with *her,* and that sort of thing never happens to Pilar and me. Usually it's only the two of us. We always sit together in class and eat together at lunch and pair up for projects. When Pilar is absent, it's a bit lonely because we only have each other.

"Yeah, sure. Sounds brilliant," Pilar says quickly. Then she turns to me, her eyes wide and frantic, in case I go and spoil it by saying no. But she can't have forgotten that Nana's outside; if I want to do anything, I'll have to ask first.

Ms. Whyte comes back into the room and hands Donna the work sheet. "Thanks, miss," Donna says. "Okay, so see you two by the bike racks in a few minutes, yeah?"

Pilar and I watch Donna leave.

"Can you believe it? Donna Taylor invited us to get french fries," Pilar says.

I put my arm around Pilar's shoulder. "Calm down. It's not like Egan Winters has asked us to go to Paris with him."

"Egan Winters? You've got to get over him, Apple. He's too old for you," Pilar says.

I shrug. "Maybe."

*　　*　　*

"There you are," Nana says. She stands up from the bench and pats me. "Do you want a juice box?"

"No thanks." I steal a look at Donna, Hazel, and Mariah who are in a huddle by the bike racks, watching.

"Good day at school?" Nana asks.

"It was fine," Pilar says. Her voice is impatient.

"Can I go to the pier for french fries?" I ask.

Nana gazes at the rain tiptoeing across the surface of the puddles. "It's a bit wet for that kind of thing."

"We won't be long. And there are five of us going, so we'd easily ward off an attacker," Pilar says.

I elbow her. She isn't helping.

Nana frowns. "How many adults?"

"Technically none. But we're all very mature," Pilar says.

"Hey! You coming?" Donna shouts across the playground. She's unlocked her bike and is pushing it toward the gates. Hazel and Mariah follow on scooters.

"*Please*, Nana." I sound whiny. I can't help it. I really want to go.

Nana examines Donna and the others. "I'm roasting lamb, and I don't want it to dry out. Come on, Apple." She marches out of the playground.

The rain pelts me.

"Quick, go and beg her," Pilar says.

"It's pointless. Her nos mean no."

Pilar pulls the belt tight on her woolen coat. "Well . . . would you mind if I went?" she asks gently. She smiles using only half her mouth. Pilar is usually a whole-mouth, whole-face smiler.

"Uh, no," I say reluctantly. I don't want her to go without me, but it wouldn't be fair to say that.

"We're going now!" Donna calls from the gates as Nana passes her.

"Are you *sure* you don't mind?" Pilar asks.

"Make up a good reason why I can't go."

35

"I'll say you have bad period pains."

"Don't say *that*."

"Okay, okay. I'll think of something good." Pilar backs away, then turns and skips to the waiting group. Donna and the other girls give her light hugs and air kisses. None of them even look my way. And then they are gone. And because it's raining, so is almost everyone else.

Everyone except Egan Winters.

He is standing outside the school with a girl. Egan is holding an umbrella over her head. She is scrolling through her phone. I watch them, wondering if they might kiss. Hoping they don't.

I know it's stupid to like Egan Winters. Pilar's got a point—he's too old. But only right now. When I'm twenty, he'll be twenty-five and that's nothing. That's normal.

All I need is for him to notice me.

"Hurry up, Apple!" Nana shouts.

Egan's eyes follow Nana's waving arm and rest on me. He squints, says something to the girl, and she laughs. Then Egan Winters laughs too.

Is he laughing at me? Is he laughing at Nana?

I pull up the hood of my rain jacket and stomp across the playground to where Nana is waiting.

"You didn't have to shout," I tell her.

"Watch your tone, young lady," Nana says, unlocking the car.

And we drive home in silence.

5

While Nana makes dinner, I lie on the couch and finish a novel by Mallary Ford. It's about a girl who falls in love with her cousin. It's good but a bit weird. And after our lamb dinner, I help Nana with the dishes before going upstairs to do my homework.

I have a page of math equations, the biology work sheet, and Mr. Gaydon's "Solitude" assignment to complete. I race through the math and biology first, to get them out of the way, then turn on the old laptop Trish handed down to me when Dad got her a shiny new one.

I write *Solitude* at the top of the document along with my name. Then I underline it and change fonts a few times. English homework is normally as easy as buttering a piece of hot toast, but instead of typing anything, my fingers hover over the keyboard like fidgety wasps.

I try hard to think about what it means to be alone. I think about what it would feel like to have no friends at all. Not even Pilar.

Then I go on Facebook.

I scroll through my newsfeed. Nothing out of the ordinary is happening except that Donna Taylor has changed her relationship status with Mariah Knox to "Engaged." The status has thirty-six likes and twenty-two comments because it is obviously a joke. Pilar, who would never usually dare contact Donna, has written a reply:

Can I be a bridesmaid?!?!?!? Xoxoxo

It must mean they had fun today at the pier. Maybe it means they're friends. Quickly, and without thinking, I type into the comments box:

Can't wait to see the wedding dress!!!!!

And I press Enter.

As soon as I do, I regret it. Donna accepted my friend request when we started in seventh grade, but she's never commented on any of *my* statuses or even liked anything I've posted. My comment sounds like I think we're friends (which we're not) and it isn't funny (which I was kind of going for). I could delete it, but if Donna has already seen the comment, she'll think it's strange if it suddenly disappears. I don't want Donna Taylor thinking I'm strange.

But if Donna *had* looked at her page in the last few seconds, she probably would have liked a few of the comments people have made about her status, which she hasn't. I decide to take the risk and delete my comment, but I don't get the chance because, at that moment, Nana taps on my bedroom door.

"Finished your homework?" she asks.

"No," I snap. If she finds out I'm on Facebook, I'll be in for an hour's lecture about how inappropriate it is. Nana thinks that the only people who use the Internet are perverts on the hunt for children.

"Well, take a break, so you can have some dessert."

"I'm not hungry," I say.

"I made apple pie." I know she baked it specially—with handfuls of chocolate chips. But I don't want any tonight. I want her to get out of my room, so I can delete my comment and not have everyone see how unpopular I am.

"I'll probably be ready in ten minutes," I say. I stare at the screen.

"Okay, I'll wait. Glass of milk with it?"

I nod. Nana closes the door.

I look at Donna's page and see that three people, including Donna, have liked Pilar's comment. My comment sits beneath it, unliked and totally stupid. I throw my head down onto the desk.

Maybe I should delete my account. Facebook is basically for showing off how pretty or popular you are. Since I'm neither, it's a bit useless.

But if I do delete my account and Mum decides to send me a friend request, she wouldn't be able to. I know she'll look me up one of these days, and when she does, I want her to be able to find me.

I hover over the settings tab when Nana calls up the stairs, "Apple, it's ready!"

*　　*　　*

"Sometimes you study too hard," Nana says as I plonk myself onto a kitchen chair. She passes me the cream in a white jug and sits down opposite. "Are the teachers overloading you?"

"No," I say. I push a piece of pie across my plate. I don't want to chit-chat. I want to scream at her and tell her that thanks to her, I now look stupid.

"Feel like watching TV with me?" Nana asks.

"I have to do my English homework," I say.

"Is something the matter, Apple?" Nana shifts in her chair. She doesn't like touchy-feely conversations. I know she wants me to tell her I'm fine.

"Can I go now?" I ask.

Nana glances at the uneaten apple pie on my plate. "Are you sick?"

My nose tingles.

Nana comes over to my side of the table where she puts her hand on my shoulder. "Why don't you call your dad tonight? I'm sure he'd like to speak to you more often," she says, not understanding, thinking this is about Dad and Trish's baby.

Beneath the table, Derry nudges my leg with his nose. I reach down and pat his head. He whines. He wants some of my pie, but Nana doesn't let me feed him at the table.

"I'll go outside with him," I say.

"It's pitch-black," Nana says.

"The stars are out," I tell her.

*   *   *

Derry cocks his leg against the shed, and I hear pee pattering against the wooden siding. The night air hums.

"Why does she have to ruin everything, Derry? If Mum

were here, she'd understand. She wouldn't treat me like a little kid every second of the day." I like having Derry to talk to. He murmurs, then sniffs around the shed.

"Apple, is that you?" a voice calls. Del's face appears through the gap in the fence. Today he's wearing a brown sweater with a dog on it. He's still in the huge rubber boots and wearing war paint.

"I'm about to go inside," I say.

"Okay. But listen, I was wondering, maybe you want to come down to the arcades with me sometime."

"Me? Uh, no thanks," I say. Even if I were allowed to go to the arcades, I wouldn't want to go with Del. I hardly know him. And what if someone saw us together?

"Suit yourself," he says, unoffended. "So who's ruining everything?"

"You were listening?"

"I was actually digging for moles, but I could hear you."

"It's nothing. Just my nan. She's paranoid I'm going to be kidnapped. She thinks I'm a baby. Anyway, forget it."

"Really? I wish my parents thought I was a baby. They make me do my own washing, which is abuse in my opinion. I'm thinking of calling the animal protection society about it."

43

"Don't you mean the children protection society?"

Del smiles.

"Oh, it was a joke," I say.

"You know, your nan might be right about you getting kidnapped. I heard on the news that you're never more than twenty meters from a killer. Or maybe it was fifty meters. Hold on, I think they said it was a predator not a killer. What's the difference?"

"That can't be true. What if you live in the countryside away from everyone?"

"Are you *serious*? The countryside's the worst for killers. They've got rivers and forests and a million other places to dump a body. And people in the country own axes and guns and, I dunno, cattle prods. That's why I hate camping."

"Apple?" Nana calls from inside.

"Come on, Derry, we've got homework to do," I say.

"What's that like?" Del asks.

"Homework?"

"I've been homeschooled all my life." That explains a lot. It definitely explains the sweaters. "I'm basically a prisoner. So will you come with me to the arcades?"

"Apple!" Nana calls again.

"Really got to go," I say and run inside. The last thing I need is to become friends with the kooky neighbor.

44

6

I log out of Facebook in case Nana decides to nose around in my laptop when I'm not here. I open a new word processing document and stare at the flashing cursor on the blank page. Then I begin my English homework.

"Solitude" by Apple Apostolopoulou

At a crowded school concert, the seats all filled with bums,
I peep out at the audience, and I think about my mum.
She should be sitting at the front and listening to me play,
But she is not here,
And is not here,
She's very far away.

Instead I have to dream of her, in America on her
    own,
Across the Atlantic Ocean, in another place,
    and another time zone.
Does she close her eyes and think of me?
Does she close her eyes and smile?
Does she plan to come home someday
To be with me,
Her only child?

I stop typing. I've written one hundred and one words, which is too many. I delete the last word. Then the one before that. Then the one before that. And I delete and delete and delete until every word is gone. I want to write something interesting and true, but I'm scared. What if Mr. Gaydon shows Nana what I've written at parents' evening? Worse, what if he makes me read it out loud in class?

I begin my homework again. I don't bother making it into a poem.

"Solitude" by Apple Apostolopoulou

Being alone is not something many people want, but

sometimes when you're alone you can achieve quite a lot. For example, I am alone now, writing this piece of homework, but if my friend Pilar were here I would probably spend the whole time talking to her and being silly and getting nothing done. Also, I wouldn't want to shower with someone else or use the toilet. Those are private things and being alone is useful when you need privacy. My dad likes to do DIY by himself. I think he likes the private thinking time, and everyone needs that.

I stop when the computer tells me I've hit one hundred words. Without proofreading the paragraph or making a single edit, I print the page. It's a boring answer. It's only half-true. But it's good enough to stop me getting a detention.

PART 2
fear

A few days later, Mr. Gaydon has marked our homework. As I guessed, he makes us read our work out
loud. I go raspberry red, partly because what I've written isn't true, partly because I know the writing is
terrible, but mainly because Mr. Gaydon makes me
stand by the whiteboard in front of the whole class,
including Donna Taylor, who yawns the whole way
through my reading.

After that he puts us into pairs and makes us edit each
other's work, which we all knew was coming. I want to
work with Pilar, but Mr. Gaydon chooses the pairings.
I'm with Linda Johns who's written about how lonely
she felt when her hamster died last summer. Pilar gets
Donna Taylor, and I can't stop looking over at them.
They laugh a lot, and at one point I catch them taking a
picture of Mr. Gaydon's bum with Donna's phone.

I'm using a green pen to correct Linda's grammar when Mrs. Tilly, the headmaster's secretary, floats into the classroom. She whispers something into Mr. Gaydon's ear. He frowns. "Could Apple please go to reception for a message from the nurse," he says. I'm sitting at the back. Everyone turns in their chairs to peer at me.

"That's you, Apple," Linda Johns says.

"Yeah," I say. I'm not sure how to act. I've never been called out of class before. Mr. Gaydon doesn't know my name, but he quickly figures out who I am and comes toward me smiling. Is it a pitying smile?

"What's the homework, sir?" I ask.

Mr. Gaydon waves away the idea of it, and my stomach drops. It must be something bad for a teacher not to care about homework. Is Dad's baby okay? Has something terrible happened to Nana?

"What's the homework?" I ask again.

Mr. Gaydon goes to his desk and comes back holding a piece of paper.

"Read this poem and write one hundred words about something you're afraid of. Again, in either poetry or prose."

"Yes, sir," I reply.

When I get to the door, I glance at Pilar, who gives me

an exaggerated thumbs-up. But it only makes me feel worse.

* * *

The school nurse is waiting by reception. "Apple," she says briskly. She leads me into an office that smells of coffee and antiseptic. She puts on her coat.

"Is it my grandmother?" I ask.

She puts her arm around me. "I'm assured it's nothing to worry about. Someone's coming to pick you up and take you to the hospital in a few minutes."

I grip the straps of my schoolbag. "What happened? Who's with her?"

"I don't have any details. Come on, let's go out to the parking lot and see if your ride's arrived."

I stand next to the nurse and can't help thinking about what would happen to me if Nana was *really* sick. Maybe they'd let me take care of her, or maybe they'd send me to live with my dad. Either way, it would be awful.

A car pulls up beside us, and a voice calls out of the window above the din of dance music, "Cab for Apple Apostolopoulou?" The person pronounces my surname perfectly.

"Thank you," the nurse says. She turns to me. "No one's been able to get in touch with your dad. Do you have a cell phone? Can you call him?"

"Yes, miss."

"Right, and if there's any problem about where you're going to sleep tonight or anything of that sort, give the school a call. Someone will be here until about six o'clock. Okay?"

"Yes, miss." I climb into the black Audi. The car pulls away, and the nurse scuttles back into reception.

I don't expect to have to talk to the driver, but as she rounds the corner she turns down the music and looks at me through the rearview mirror. She can see me fully. I can only see her eyes—rusty brown and heavily made up. "Everything okay, honey?" she asks.

"Fine, thank you," I say sourly because Nana has always warned me not to talk to strangers—although if the driver is a kidnapper, there isn't a lot I can do about it now I'm strapped into the backseat of her car.

"Your grandmother is fine," the woman says. Her eyes crinkle into a smile. The car turns into a cul-de-sac and slows to a stop. I stiffen. Is she planning to abduct me in broad daylight? And how does she know about Nana?

"I'm supposed to be going to the h-hospital," I stutter. I grasp the door handle and wonder whether to jump out and make a run for it.

The woman turns fully so her whole face is revealed. She smiles again. Her teeth are perfectly straight and white. "It's me, Apple," she says gently.

My mouth goes dry. It can't be. But it is. "Mum?" I only recognize her because I've studied the photos she's e-mailed to Nana.

"Phew. I was worried for a second you didn't recognize me. You look so different."

I try to think of something to say. Something that will mark this as an important moment in our lives. Before I can think of anything, Mum gets out of the car, opens the back door, and smiles again, with her lovely American teeth.

"How long are you staying?" is all I can say.

"I'm back for good, sweetheart." For good? Meaning *forever*? A few moments earlier I was terrified of my life changing, and it was, but in the best possible way. "I know it's probably a bit of a shock seeing me, but can I have a hug?" Mum says. I jump out of the car and throw my arms around her. I breathe in her heavy perfume. I can hardly believe she's real.

"Mum," I say.

"So what should we do with our afternoon?" she asks.

I shrug. And then I remember Nana. "Shouldn't we go to the hospital?"

She laughs into the sky. "What? No! That was to get you out of school, you ninny. Nana's fine. I think."

"Have you seen her?"

"I'll see her later. Right now, I'm hungry. Aren't you?" she asks.

It's almost lunchtime. I only had a few spoons of porridge for breakfast. "Very," I say.

Mum tugs the band holding her ponytail together and shakes her long hair loose. It falls in smooth waves down her back. "Right, hop in the front and let's get going."

I want to ask her if Nana knows I'm missing school, but it's a silly question. So I don't say anything. I climb into the passenger seat next to her and fasten my seat belt.

8

The Palace Hotel sits at the top of the cliffs. Not that they're proper cliffs with scary death-drops. The cliffs in Brampton-on-Sea roll into the ocean like a soft blanket. Sailing boats are dots in the distance. The clouds are creamy against the horizon.

The hotel is where the posh weddings and mayors' banquets are held. And here I am sitting at one of their tables by the window with a stiff napkin on my lap and a plate of battered fish called calamari on the plate in front of me. *And* I'm with my mum.

"Well, go on, have a taste. It's very common in America," Mum says.

I dip a piece of calamari into tomatoey sauce and pop it into my mouth. It's rubbery but good. I reach for more.

"Told you you'd like it," Mum says. She pushes her

white wine toward me. I take a sip and giggle. I feel sort of light-headed, but I don't know if it's because of the wine or how excited I am to be with my mum. She takes back her glass and guzzles down the last bit. Then she holds it up for the waiter to see. He scutters off to fetch another. "Nothing like a chilled glass of chardonnay," she says.

She gazes out at the sea.

The tide is in. Waves crash against the cliffs in thick, noisy gulps. Mum stares for a few minutes, and I watch her, not saying anything.

The waiter places the wine on the table between us. Without taking her eyes from the sea, Mum reaches for the glass and sips. She doesn't really resemble other mums: she's wearing loads of chunky necklaces over a thin T-shirt. And her nose is pierced.

"When I was your age, I had a boyfriend called Glen. He was four years older than me, and I used to sneak down to the seafront with him. He always had money for beer. That's naughty, isn't it?" She looks at me like she expects me to say something. I try to think of what she wants to hear. Then she yawns, so I pop another piece of calamari into my mouth and chew. "How is it living with Nana?"

"Nice. Okay. She's a bit strict."

Mum snorts. "Nothing changes there. She used to make me miserable."

"It's better than living with Dad. Then I'd have to see his new wife every day. Her name's Trish. I hate her."

Mum laughs. "I think there's a law that you're supposed to hate your stepmother!"

"I guess." I push a piece of calamari across my plate. It's too much to finish.

"Want dessert? I'm having a piece of the warm chocolate fudge cake."

"That sounds lovely," I say, still hardly able to believe I'm really with my mum. This is the best day of my life.

Ever.

9

Eventually Mum and I have to go back to Nana's house, and when we get through the door, it's like jumping into a box of exploding fireworks.

Nana sends me straight upstairs, where I burrow beneath my duvet to try to drown out the sound of Nana screaming. Derry nuzzles my neck. It doesn't help. I can still hear them.

Nana: How dare you take her out of school without telling me! I was out of my mind with worry. I thought she'd been abducted, for God's sake. I called the hospital *and* the police.

Mum: I have a right to see my own child.

Nana: Since when? Five hours ago? You stroll into her life like the last eleven years haven't even happened. I won't have you hurting her, do you hear me?

Mum: We were having fun. She's happy. Go and ask her.

Nana: I'm sure she is, Annie. But that might be because she's fourteen years old and you took her *drinking*. Do you think that's how a mother behaves?

Mum: She had a few sips.

Nana: And I suppose that makes it okay?

Mum: I'm sorry, but I'm back in Brampton for good, and I want a relationship with her. I hope you can support that.

Nana: How dare you? I've spent years trying to persuade you to take an interest in Apple.

Mum: I've always been interested in her. I've had . . . things to sort out. I couldn't be what she needed. But I'm here for her now. I'm not eighteen anymore. I can be a mother. I *am* a mother. And not a bad one.

Derry sniffs my armpit. "Get off." I push him away. Why am I hiding upstairs and not with Mum, defending her? If I let Nana keep shouting, maybe she'll persuade Mum to run away again. I don't want that.

I fly down the stairs, closely followed by Derry. Mum is sitting at the kitchen table. Nana is towering over her.

"Leave Mum alone!" I shout.

"I told you to wait in your room," Nana says sternly. Any other time I would scurry away. Not today.

Mum's mascara is smudged, and her eyes are red from crying.

And then the front door opens and is slammed shut. Derry barks, growls, and backs himself into a corner.

"Bernadette? Apple?" It's Dad. Nana must have been so worried she called him. And he came. He actually came.

He charges into the kitchen, smashing the door against the fridge. Mum jumps up. When Dad sees her, he gasps and drops his phone.

"Chris. Hi. You're looking good," Mum says. Her hair falls over one eye and she smiles. She's so pretty. I wish she would steal Dad away from Trish.

"We thought she'd been bloody well kidnapped. Now I see *you're* behind this. Why didn't I guess?" Dad folds his arms across his chest. He glares at Mum. He's not flirting with her, I can tell that much.

Mum tries to look sorry. "I didn't mean to have anyone running to the priest to arrange a funeral. I wanted to see her. I got off the plane, and I couldn't wait."

Dad keeps his arms folded, but his expression softens. "You flew in today?"

"This morning. I just finished a show."

Dad smiles. Nana's mouth is puckered into a sour pout.

"That's lovely, Annie. I do hope your adoring audience gave you a standing ovation," Nana says. "I'm wondering what the plan is now. Are you going to tap dance on the pier for money?"

Mum stands up and puts on her coat. "I have to go now. I've appointments this evening to see some two-bed apartments. I'm hoping that Apple . . ." She pauses and takes a deep breath. "I want Apple to come and live with me."

Nana's eyes become hot clots of rage. Dad winces like he's been pinched. But no one speaks. I can't even think. I feel dizzy as the blood stutters around my heart. Live with her? In a place that isn't Nana's house?

"The truth is, Apple isn't happy," Mum says. "Isn't that right, Apple?"

Nana pulls her hands out of her pockets. Is she going to hit Mum?

"Apple told me that you basically treat her like a prisoner, and that Chris is wrapped up in his new wife and life. I want to give her more."

Dad and Nana turn to me. My face flushes. Why is Mum telling them what I've said? It wasn't meant to be broadcast.

"Is this true, Apple?" Nana's eyes tighten into thin lines.

I pick at the skin around my nails. Maybe if I do this for a while everyone will ignore me and continue fighting with each other. They wait for me to speak.

"I don't need to be collected from school," I murmur.

"Trish has only ever been kind to you, Apple," Dad says.

"It's okay, Apple," Mum says. She gets up from the table, stands behind me, and places her hands on my shoulders. She's on my side, and Nana and Dad seem to be on the other.

Derry cowers in his basket. He can tell something horrible is happening. I want to snuggle with him, so we'll both feel better.

"I don't need an answer now, of course. Apple will need a few days to decide what she'd like to do," Mum says.

Nana slams her fist on the kitchen table. "Apple is staying with *me*. I won't even discuss it."

"If she wants to be with me, no court would prevent

it," Mum says quietly, and although I'm not entirely sure what this means, it makes Nana wobble and I wish Mum hadn't said it.

"I think you should go," Dad snaps. He grabs Mum's studded leather handbag from the back of one of the kitchen chairs and flings it at her.

You'd never know Mum was in the middle of an argument. She seems to be smirking. "You have a think about it, Apple, okay? Decide for yourself."

I nod dumbly.

"Get out!" Dad shouts.

"And remember that I love you," Mum adds.

A marble rises in my throat.

"I know you do," I say. But until today, I had no idea.

10

Nana and Dad sit downstairs whispering. It's obvious they are plotting against Mum. I don't even try to over-hear—I don't want to know what they're saying. To dis-tract myself from having to think about it, I root in my schoolbag for my English homework. I find the poem Mr. Gaydon gave me this morning and read through it.

It's a poem called "Stevie Scared" about a boy who is scared of everything, and it's sort of funny because he's even scared of things like ladders and trees. But my favorite part of the poem is the last bit where we find out that Stevie is so afraid of the world that he hurts people to prove how tough he is; he acts mean so no one will ever know he's a scaredy-cat.

I wonder how the poem could relate to my life. But Stevie is not me. When I'm scared, I don't fight with people—I shrivel up.

I start typing.

"Apple Afraid" by Apple Apostolopoulou

Apple Afraid, afraid of fights,
Afraid of Christmas, of thundery nights,
Afraid of butterflies, afraid of slugs,
Afraid of Nana's kisses, afraid of Dad's hugs,
Afraid of circuses, afraid of clowns,
Afraid of Dad's moods, afraid of Nana's frowns,
Afraid of speaking in front of the class,
Afraid of being made to look like an ass,
Afraid of having no friends at school,
Afraid of all the girls who are easily cool,
Afraid to be honest, afraid to be true,
Afraid of Mum turning up out of the blue,
Afraid of drowning, swallowing water,
Afraid of being a lousy daughter.

I check the word count: one hundred words exactly. I cup my chin in my hand and think about printing it and handing it in. I haven't the energy to write another fake answer. But then there's the problem of Mr. Gaydon asking us to read aloud and edit one another's work. If he let us work with our friends and I knew Pilar would read it, that would be okay. But he could pair me with anyone. I could get Jim Joyce, for God's sake.

I sigh and open a new document.

"Derry" by Apple Apostolopoulou

My dog, Derry, is usually very sweet and obedient. But when I take him for a walk on the lead, he gets all excited and tries to break my arm. And the scariest part is when he sees another dog, especially a big one like a Rottweiler, because Derry doesn't realize he's only a soppy Labrador. He starts by sniffing the Rottweiler's bum. Then they do this dance where they go around and around in circles until Derry barks angrily and so does the other dog and there's chaos. I worry Derry will get killed in a dogfight someday.

I press Print. The paper stammers out of the printer. I need to make a bigger effort with my English homework but not tonight. I have other things to think about, and doing well at school isn't one of them.

11

"I like your nana," Pilar says. "I'd stay with her." We've eaten lunch and are sitting on the tennis court behind the gym, sharing a bag of licorice. It's drizzling. No one else is around.

"Nana's so strict all the time."

"But why was your mum in America anyway?" Pilar asks.

"She's an actress," I say. I puff with pride.

"Couldn't she come back for holidays?"

"She was always busy."

"My uncle lives in California, and he said that in America you don't get any holidays. I mean, he gets Christmas Day off, but there's not even any such thing as Boxing Day. He works on Saturdays too."

"I don't know how much she worked," I admit.

Pilar's phone vibrates, and she checks it.

"Who's that?" I ask.

"No one."

Is she trying to keep secrets from me? I poke her. "What do you mean 'no one'?"

"It's Donna. She said she wants to tell me something when we get to history later."

"Hold on. You two are actually friends now?" I ask.

Pilar pulls another licorice stick from the packet. She twists it around her index finger until the tip turns red. "I think so. She's nice. Not one bit snobby like you thought."

"I never said she was snobby."

Pilar bites the purple tip of her finger. "Have you seen *E.T.*?"

"No," I say sharply. Talking about films isn't going to help me make a decision about where to live. And I'm annoyed she's suddenly chummy with Donna Taylor but I'm not.

"Well, E.T. is this creature who comes from another planet," Pilar says.

"Yeah, I know that."

"All right, all right. Anyway, E.T. comes down and meets this boy called Elliott who's lonely and stuff, and he really loves Elliott and they have fun together

70

and everything but then, at the end—spoiler alert—he goes back to space because that's where he's supposed to be. It isn't safe on Earth." Pilar raises her eyebrows.

Is the story supposed to mean something? I shake my head. She throws up her arms, exasperated.

"Oh, come on. Your mum is obviously like E.T. She really loved America and everything, but there's no place like home, is there?"

"That's the wrong film you're thinking of. It's Dorothy from *The Wizard of Oz* who says 'there's no place like home.'"

"But you get my point," Pilar says.

The bell rings for the end of lunch. Pilar jumps up. I stay where I am.

Pilar takes off toward 200 Block and double French. "Come on!" she shouts.

Puddles are forming in the dips in the playground. The rain is more than a drizzle now.

I imagine I am wearing red rubber boots. If I were, and I could bump them together and find myself in either Nana's house or Mum's, where would I go? What would I wish for?

"There's no place like home," I say aloud. I think of Nana, her mouth bent into an angry grimace.

"There's no place like home," I say again. I think of Mum's beautiful American smile.

"There's no place like home," I say one last time. I close my eyes. I bump my heels together. When I open my eyes, I'm still at school.

And I'm no closer to knowing where home is.

"Hurry up, Apple! *Nous sommes* going to be *trop tard*," Pilar shouts.

I stuff the licorice into my blazer pocket and follow Pilar to class.

12

When Nana and I get home from school that evening, Mum is sitting on our front steps eating a scone. "Hey, guys!" she says. She jumps up. Crumbs fall from her denim skirt. She's got leopard-print tights on under it.

"What do you want?" Nana asks.

"Hi, Mum!" I say. I go to her and she kisses both my cheeks.

"I've found an apartment in a good neighborhood. I wondered if Apple wanted to come over for dinner. I've someone I'd like her to meet."

"I'd love to come," I say.

Nana clicks her tongue. She takes my hand and forces me to stand behind her as though Mum's a bomb that could detonate at any second. "I've baked salmon for dinner. I don't like waste."

"How about after dinner then?" Mum asks.

"Apple has homework to do and she has school

tomorrow, in case you'd forgotten," Nana says. She is careful not to say no outright.

"Okay." Mum nibbles on a fingernail. "How about the weekend?"

"Apple practices her clarinet at the weekends."

"Not for the whole weekend," I say. I peep out from behind Nana. Mum tilts her head to the side and smiles. My insides bubble. I still can't believe she's back. I keep expecting I'll wake up from a dream or Nana will sit me down and break the news that Mum's gone again.

"Sunday?" Mum asks.

"You can fetch her at one o'clock after we've been to Mass, but you're to have her back before five, so she can get ready for the week," Nana says. She marches up the steps, past Mum, and roughly unlocks the front door. "Come inside please, Apple." I do as I'm told. Nana leaves Mum there on the steps like some criminal we need to be afraid of.

"Can't she come in?" I ask.

Mum tucks her hair behind her ears, which have three piercings apiece. "It's all right, Apple."

"No, it isn't all right. It's my house too," I say.

"Go upstairs and do your homework," Nana says.

"Go on, Apple. I'll see you on Sunday."

I don't want to, but I stomp up to my room. I open the window and look out. I can only see the tops of Mum's and Nana's heads.

I can hear everything.

Mum: I told you I was sorry.

Nana: Eleven years, Annie. That is how long I have waited to hear you say it.

Mum: Can you let me try to make it up to you? I have someone I want you to meet. An important someone.

Nana: I don't think so. Apple's had quite enough of that kind of thing from her father.

Mum: What? Oh yeah, I see what you mean. So Chris got married eventually. I don't know why, but it makes me sad.

Nana: Could we avoid the melodrama, if possible, Annie? Now don't you be late on Sunday.

Nana disappears inside. The door bangs. Mum shuffles down the steps.

When she's at the bottom, she looks up at the house and sees me. I wave, and she waves back. And I start wondering how it would be if I never had to wave good-bye anymore. I start thinking it would be really nice.

13

The first thing Mum and I do on Sunday afternoon is make a stop at the Palace Hotel. I've had lunch, so Mum orders me a vanilla milkshake and a fudge brownie. She eats a pear-and-goat-cheese salad. We talk about TV and books and school—things I can't speak to Nana about because Nana's only hobbies are going to church and watching cookery programs.

"Donna Taylor thinks she's something then, does she?" Mum asks, her eyes wide, so I know she's interested.

"Sort of."

"And why's that?"

"Well, she's pretty and she wears nice shoes and makeup and she seems older," I say.

"What? But *you're* pretty, and getting shoes and makeup isn't a big deal."

"Nana won't buy me any makeup and we get my shoes from Clarks, so yes, it is a big deal," I tell her.

Mum shudders as though I've said something frightening. "We're going shopping!" she says, and summons the waiter.

*   *   *

In town I try on about a hundred pairs of shoes—red ones, gold ones, a pair of platforms covered in diamonds, and loads of others that I would never wear. Mum makes me pose, stretched across the seats in the shoe shop, then takes funny pictures with her camera phone. Even when the shop assistant mutters something about time-wasters, Mum doesn't care: she sticks out her tongue at the assistant behind her back, which makes me fall down on the floor laughing.

I finally find a pair I love—brown ballet shoes with golden buckles across the toes. Mum doesn't even ask the price. She tells the shop assistant to ring them up and hands her a credit card.

"They're sixty pounds," I whisper to Mum.

"Good. We'll have plenty of money left for makeup," she says, and winks.

*   *   *

Mum lets me choose anything I want from the makeup counter as long as it isn't tested on animals. So I get a tube of foundation, a blackest-black mascara, some pink blusher, and a packet of tinted lip glosses. Mum also grabs some green plastic-rimmed sunglasses, which she says I'm to wear even in the winter—if I don't want to get lines around my eyes.

By four thirty I'm so happy it could be Christmas—how I always imagined Christmas *should* feel.

Driving home, Mum doesn't stop at pedestrian crossings, and she whizzes through roundabouts, hardly checking for other cars, all to make it back on time. Which we do.

We pull up outside Nana's house at exactly four fifty-nine.

"I guess we're home," she says, cutting the engine.

Even though I've had a perfect day, I feel like someone has suddenly thrown a bucket of sadness all over me, and I am dripping from it. I sit peering at my ragged finger-nails.

"What's wrong, Apple?"

Every time I say good-bye to Mum I worry it will be the last time I see her. "I just . . . I wish . . . ," I begin. But I don't know how to tell Mum what I'm feeling in case she thinks it means I don't trust her—that I'm like Nana and believe she'll run away again.

She pats my knee. "You know you can call me anytime you like. And if you come and live with me, we can have lots of fun days like today. And next time I'll take you to the apartment. I planned on it today, but we seem to have been sidetracked." She points at the bags by my feet. "Actually, you might want to keep some of that stuff hidden from you-know-who."

I nod. Nana would be furious if she found out Mum had bought me makeup. And I'm not sure why, but I have a feeling she'd object to the sunglasses and shoes too.

I look up at the house. Everything about it is Nana: the neat window boxes; the clean, white-net curtains; the tidy lawn. But which part of it is me?

Nana appears at the front door. She is scowling and wringing her hands in a tea towel.

"You'd better go inside," Mum says.

* * *

The clock ticktocks on the mantelpiece. Nana and I sit opposite each other eating. Nana chews loudly. I push the cabbage, potatoes, and lamb around my plate.

Nana takes a gulp of water. "If there's something on your mind, you might as well spit it out." She taps her fingers impatiently against the tablecloth. She doesn't really want to talk. And I don't know what to say. My mind is all tangled up with wanting Mum and loving her and not understanding why Nana won't give her a chance.

I shrug.

"I don't like you doing that, Apple, it's rude. Use words please," Nana says.

"I'm *fine*," I say.

"Well, I won't have you sulking. Either speak up or cheer up."

I throw my fork down. Nana flinches. "I want you to be nicer to Mum," I snap. "She's your daughter. She's my mum. And I want her around. Can't you be nicer?"

Nana crosses her arms over her chest. "Your mother ran off to be an actress. I don't respect that," she says.

"She was in plays. She was living her *dream*."

"She was prancing around on stage wanting to be adored by people who didn't know her while her own family spent years waiting for her to come home. Some dream."

Nana has a point. Why wasn't our love enough for Mum? It's a question I don't want to think about. "But you're religious. You're supposed to forgive. The priest says so," I tell her.

Nana looks ashamed, but for no more than a second.

"Will you dry, if I wash? I don't want to run the dishwasher for a handful of plates," she says. She marches to the sink.

I follow her and tip my uneaten dinner into the bin. "Are you okay, Nana?" I ask.

"When have I not been okay?" She throws the plastic washing-up bowl into the basin and turns on both taps. Whether I like it or not, the gushing water drowns out all other questions.

Mr. Gaydon doesn't make me read out my homework, but he does make Pilar read hers. She's written about flying, how when you get to a certain altitude the airplane's engines go quiet, like they've been switched off, and it makes you think you're going to end up splattered across a field in France: one leg in a tree, one in a cow pat.

"Flying is a common fear," Mr. Gaydon says, "so thank you, Pilar, for sharing it with us." Mr. Gaydon writes the word *fear* on the board and underlines it twice, like Ms. Savage did with words she wanted us to learn to spell.

He rubs his chin. "Where do fears come from?" he asks. Mackenzie Bainbridge has been sitting at the front since Mr. Gaydon started teaching us. Her hand shoots up. Mr. Gaydon reaches forward and puts it down. He continues. "Pilar is scared of flying, but is it really the flying part that frightens her, or could it be something else? Think about what you've written. Is there something behind the fear? Like an even deeper terror? One we all share?"

He pauses, and Mackenzie puts up her hand again. Mr. Gaydon ignores it even though it is practically in his face. "Read your piece again. I bet that most of you have revealed something about human nature in your writing. Think hard."

I look at my homework. I didn't hand in the true answer I'd written, so I don't expect to find any deeper feelings in the paragraph about Derry. But then I get to thinking that what I really hate about Derry sniffing dogs' bums is not knowing how he's going to react. Or how the other dog will react.

A few kids have their hands up. Mr. Gaydon calls on Donna.

"We're all afraid of dying. I wrote about snakes, and I think they could strangle me. Pilar thinks she could end up dead from flying. So . . . death." Donna smiles and so does Mr. Gaydon.

"That's very interesting," he says. "Death is a universal fear. How many of you think your fear is linked to dying?"

About half the class raise their hands, basically all the girls, including Pilar. I don't. Donna glances at me.

"So for the rest of you, what can the fear be if not the fear of death?" Mr. Gaydon asks.

The room is quiet.

I feel Mr. Gaydon watching me.

"Do you have something to say, Apple?" he asks.

The class is gawking. "Maybe it's . . . maybe it's control. Like I hate it when I can't control my dog. And when Pilar's flying she's out of control because she can't fly the plane. And . . ." I look over at Donna. I don't know how snakes make her feel out of control, and I don't want to guess in case I offend her. She already looks a bit annoyed.

Mr. Gaydon claps his hands together. "I like that. Who here has a fear that is linked to being out of control?" For a minute, no one puts up their hand. I feel stupid. But then Mackenzie raises hers. And then Karl Woods and then Iona Churchill and then more and more people, until almost everyone has a hand in the air.

"Wow! I didn't expect such consensus," Mr. Gaydon says.

I blush because everyone is looking at me again.

The bell rings. We fidget. "Good work today, folks. See

you tomorrow," Mr. Gaydon says, giving us permission to pile out of the classroom into the heaving corridor.

Pilar and I are by the lockers when Donna, Hazel, and Mariah stop next to us. Donna whispers something to Pilar, and they laugh.

"What's funny?" I ask.

"Oh, nothing. You had to be there," Donna says.

"Where did you have to be?" I ask.

Pilar fiddles with her gold stud earring.

"We went swimming on Sunday and there were these guys there who . . . ," Donna begins, but she can't continue because she is laughing again. Uncontrollably.

"You went swimming together?" I ask. Pilar didn't tell me. She certainly didn't invite me.

"We all did," Mariah says.

"And then for kebabs," Hazel adds.

"I didn't ask you because I knew your nan would've said you couldn't come," Pilar says. She examines the floor.

"And it's always awkward with odd numbers," Donna says.

"I was busy on Sunday anyway," I tell them.

"Church?" Pilar asks. She's forgotten I told her I was meeting Mum. She's forgotten how important it was to me. And she hasn't even noticed my new shoes, which I slipped on once Nana had dropped me off.

"Yeah, church," I say.

"Shall we get lunch, Pilar?" Donna asks. She doesn't look at me, so I know I'm not invited, and I expect Pilar to tell Donna that she always eats with me—that it's the two of us at school and no one else.

"You hungry, Apple?" Pilar asks uncomfortably.

Donna sighs. Hazel rolls her eyes. Mariah walks away.

"No," I say. "I'm not sure what's happened to my appetite lately."

Donna's eyes rest on my belly. "Well, it's never a bad thing to lose a few pounds," she says.

I swallow hard and open my locker door to hide my face.

"I'll see you later then," Pilar says.

"Yeah, see you," I say.

And she is gone.

15

I know that Pilar isn't my wife or anything. She's allowed to have other friends. But I can't help feeling jittery with jealousy. I spend all lunch period pacing the corridors and wondering how I'll win her back from Donna. Pilar's my only friend. If I lose her, I'll have no one.

So I come up with a speech; when I get to drama, I'll be honest and tell her how I feel. We're performing a sketch together; she'll have to partner up with me and listen.

But when I get into the theater, Pilar is already sitting with Donna, Hazel, and Mariah. There's no way I'll get a chance to tell her how I feel now. I'll be alone all lesson. Everyone will stare and wonder why Pilar and I have fallen out. I don't want anyone knowing I've got no friends.

Without waiting another second, I scan the theater to

make sure Ms. Court isn't hiding somewhere and make a run for it. I can hide out in some toilets until school finishes, then meet Nana in the playground as usual—no one needs to know I skipped a couple of lessons.

I sprint across the playground and into the girls' toilets of 100 Block. Two eleventh graders are brushing their hair. A girl with blond waves to her waist presses her lips against a mirror, leaving a bright-pink kiss on it. Her friend in a miniskirt and ripped tights lights up a cigarette.

"Want a puff?" she asks.

"No, thank you," I say, edging into a stall. I lock it and sit on the toilet without bothering to put down the seat.

"Hey, titch," one of the girls calls. "You'll be late for your lesson if you stay in there."

"Leave her alone, Mags. Maybe she ate something spicy."

The toilets echo with laughter, and then a door rattles and it's quiet.

I can't stay here for two whole lessons, not if eleventh graders are going to be coming in and out and smoking and shouting at me the whole time. Maybe I could go to the office and say I'm sick. But the nurse would probably call Nana, who would take one look at me and know I was lying. They might even send me back to class.

Only one person would understand. I reach into my bag for my phone.

Mum: Hello, yes?

Me: Mum?

Mum: Who is it?

Me: Mum, it's me, Apple.

Mum: Apple! Hey! I was wondering when you were going to call. Are you okay?

Me: I hope you aren't busy. You're probably doing something important. I don't want to—

Mum: Busy? No! No, not really. What's up?

Me: Nothing.

Mum: Tell me.

Me: My friend Pilar went off with that girl Donna Taylor I was telling you about, so I . . . I have no one to hang around with and it's embarrassing and . . .

Mum: Apple?

Me: I'm sorry I called you. It sounds silly.

Mum: Where are you now? You aren't hiding out in the toilets, are you?

Me: . . .

Mum: Do you want me to come and get you?

Me: I only have two lessons left today.

Mum: But do you want to leave?

Me: Yes.

Mum: Right. Go to reception and say you've got a stomachache. Give me fifteen minutes.

Me: What about Nana?

Mum: What about her?

The receptionist isn't pleased to see me. "What's wrong exactly?"

"My stomach hurts," I say.

"Do you have PE now?" she asks.

"No, miss."

"Math?"

"No, miss."

"Right, well, the nurse isn't here today, and you can't hang around the office. Can someone pick you up?"

"My mum can get me," I say, quickly adding, "I'll call her."

The receptionist slides the window open wide enough to push a clipboard at me. A pen dangles on a string by its side. "Sign out," she says.

* * *

When Mum pulls up outside reception, she pushes open the passenger door and waves. "Hurry up, babes. I gotta be at the bank in five minutes."

As I am clicking my seat belt into place, Mum leans over and kisses me on the ear.

"So tell me what happened," she says. She races out of the school gates. The car tires screech against the road.

"Pilar, who's supposed to be my best friend, has dumped me for Donna Taylor," I tell her.

"Why?"

"I don't know. I think it's because I'm not allowed out and stuff."

"Pilar doesn't sound like much of a friend to me. She sounds like a bitch," Mum says. I laugh. Nana would never say something like that—she would tell me to stop being silly. And she would never, *ever* swear in front of me.

"I don't know if she is. Deep down I think she's nice," I say. Pilar's been my friend since I started secondary school. It's the first time she's been mean. And she hasn't even really been mean; she's just leaving me out. I'm not sure whether or not that counts. "Donna

Taylor's got loads of friends. Why does she have to have mine too?"

"Donna Taylor? What a name. She sounds like a stripper."

"She's really popular," I say.

Mum smiles. "Strippers usually are. Anyway, so what? Anyone can be popular."

"I can't," I say.

"Really?" Mum says. She tries to cover up a smile with her fingers, but I think she might be plotting something.

* * *

After Mum and I have gone to the bank, dropped off some dry cleaning, and stopped for an ice cream, Mum takes me home. She doesn't come in with me. "I'm late. I've got to scoot off. But I'll see you soon, okay?" she says.

Nana is in the hall, lacing up her shoes. She does a double take when she sees me. Derry bounds out of the kitchen and noses my schoolbag. I ruffle his fur, and his tail wags.

"You got out early? Why didn't you call? I don't like you taking the bus alone," Nana says.

I could make something up, but I've never lied to Nana. Even the thought of it makes my neck go blotchy. "I fell out with Pilar," I say.

"What does that mean?"

"I told the receptionist I was sick. Mum picked me up."

Nana opens the front door, but Mum is gone. She keeps her back to me and hangs up her coat on the hall stand along with her red head scarf. "This is not acceptable, Apple."

"What isn't acceptable?"

Nana turns around. "The school shouldn't have let you leave. I'm your legal guardian."

"But she's my *mum*," I say.

"And she believed that a tiff with Pilar was a good reason to pull you out of lessons?"

"Pilar's ditched me, Nana. I've got no one now. Donna Taylor took her away."

Nana rolls her eyes. "Can't you all be friends together?"

"No, we can't. That isn't how it works. Donna's leaving me out on purpose. She doesn't like me."

Nana puts her hands on her hips. "Why wouldn't she like you?"

"Because I'm never allowed to do anything. Why

wouldn't you let me go with her and her friends after school? Now she's stolen Pilar."

"So tell Pilar you're upset."

I pull off my schoolbag and toss it at the bottom of the stairs. "You aren't listening!" I shout. "You never *listen*. All you do is tell me I'm wrong and silly and young."

Derry's tail stops wagging. He slides back into the kitchen. He's such a wimp.

"Apple, you know we don't shout like that in this house."

But I can't stop myself. "We don't shout and we don't talk. You just tell me what to do all the time!"

"I'm trying to take care of you."

"I'm fourteen, and you think I'm eight. It's your fault I have no friends."

Nana freezes. "What's happened? You aren't behaving like yourself." She doesn't even try to think about what she's done. She can't imagine she's wrong. It has to be me. It always has to be my fault, just like it's always been Mum's fault for leaving.

I push my shoulders back and swallow. I feel brave and scared all at once. "I don't want to live here anymore," I tell her.

94

"What did you say?" Nana glares at me. I might as well have slapped her.

I turn and head up to my bedroom.

"Apple, get back down here," Nana calls after me.

"I'm going to live with Mum," I say, and shut my bedroom door.

16

Dad is in Nana's kitchen the next morning. "I'm missing work to be here," he says.

I make myself a bowl of cornflakes while Dad tries to convince me to stay with Nana. He says things like, "Your mother isn't what she seems," and "I don't want you to look back and regret that you did this." And when I tell him that Mum's really trying, Dad goes quiet and says, "Well, it's about bloody well time."

Even though Dad doesn't want me to live with Mum, he never says I should live with him. Trish wouldn't allow it. Anyway, I'd rather live under a bridge with diseased rats than in a house with Trish—but he could at least offer.

Then Nana and Derry are back from their walk, and Mum is at the front door, and I am dragging my suitcase down the path. It is all happening so quickly. Quicker than I imagined.

Derry sits on the front step. He is confused. I kneel in front of him and put my face into his neck. "Take care of Nana," I tell him. "Don't forget to bark at strangers, okay?"

Derry looks at Nana. She is standing with her hands in the pocket of her apron. She is watching Mum pack up the car. She is not looking at me.

I know she's sad. So am I. But Nana's solution for everything is either to feed me or to get angry.

"Do you have everything you need?" she asks in a croaky whisper. Her eyes are hard.

"I think so. But I can come back and get anything I forgot, can't I?" I ask. My room is still packed with all my stuff because Mum doesn't have a lot of space in her new flat. I've left my posters on the walls and my drawers full of summer clothes.

Nana nods. "You know you can come back anytime, Apple."

Mum taps the face of her watch and waves for me to get into the car.

I want to tell Nana how grateful I am that she let me live with her all my life. I want to tell her that, even though I've never said it out loud before, I really do love her. But when I try to speak, I end up coughing. Nana pats me on the back.

"Go on now, if that's what you're doing," she says.

Derry rests his head between Nana's feet. His big brown eyes are watery.

"See you soon, Derry," I say.

I quickly turn around and rush toward Mum. If I linger, I might change my mind. And Nana doesn't wait at the door. She doesn't wave me off like she usually does when visitors leave.

She shuts the door gently and is gone.

17

Mum pushes open the front entrance and kicks junk mail off the mat. Two doors separate the house into flats. Mum opens a red one with scuff marks along the bottom and drags my suitcase up a flight of narrow stairs.

"Here we are. Come on," she says. She huffs as she plonks the case by the stairwell. She sweeps her arms wide. "Home, sweet home," she says. We are in a large sitting room with a small kitchen tucked into one corner. Piles of boxes, like giant building blocks, are scattered around the room, and the couch, the only piece of furniture in the room apart from a tiny dining table, is covered in clothes.

Dust dances by the open windows. The room smells of burned toast.

"What do you think?" Mum asks.

"It's got loads of potential," I say as cheerfully as I

can. It doesn't look like a home yet, but she's just moved in.

Mum smiles. "Exactly. Loads of potential. We'll get some pictures up and maybe paint the walls. It'll be unrecognizable. I love the open-plan living, don't you? Makes me feel like I'm still in the States."

Mum goes to the kitchen. She rummages in a box and pulls out a saucepan. She fills it with water and places it on the stove.

"Let's have coffee."

"Okay," I say.

"But I want to give you the full tour first. I think you'll be surprised," she says. She opens her handbag, which is slung across her body, and takes out a packet of cigarettes. She pinches one between her lips and lights the end, drawing in deeply and exhaling the smoke through her nose.

"You smoke," I say.

Mum pulls the cigarette out of her mouth and looks at it. "I know. Disgusting. I meant to give up in the New Year, but it never happened." She laughs and inhales again. She goes to the open window and blows the smoke outside. She swats the air with her free hand. When she's finished her cigarette, I follow her to the hallway.

She pushes open the first door, revealing a pink bathroom. The side of the bath and sink are crowded with bottles of shampoo, soaps, and makeup. "Little girls' room," Mum says. "And this is my room." She opens the door opposite. "Thinking of painting it a duck-egg blue. And I like butterflies, so maybe one side of wallpaper. What do you think?"

"That would be nice," I say.

Mum pulls her bedroom door behind her. "A bit of a mess, but I'll get there."

At the end of the hallway is one more door. Mum is beaming. "And this is *your* room." She turns the handle.

I step inside and almost screech with excitement. Instead of a single bed in the corner and a large sensible desk, like at Nana's, Mum's bought a yellow bunk bed and two green beanbags. "It's so fun!" I say.

"Phew! I was worried you'd think it looked childish. But I thought better a bunk bed than two separate beds squished in."

"Huh?"

I feel something coming. I don't want to hear it. I don't want to know. I put my hands in my pockets and make fists.

"Rain? Rain, are you awake, my darling?" Mum says.

The covers on the top bunk shift, and from beneath them a head appears. A red head with frayed pigtails, curly at the ends.

The tired eyes of a kid.

A girl.

She rubs her eyes with her fists.

"This is Apple. I was telling you all about her, remember? You're going to be best friends, I know it," Mum says.

The girl sits up and blinks. She finds a pair of large round glasses under her pillow and slips them over her nose. "Hi," Rain says.

I don't reply. I'm just about managing to stay on my feet.

"Apple?" Mum says. Her voice sounds like it's coming from another room. From behind a wall. "Apple?"

"Yes?" I look at her, fixing my mouth into a jagged smile.

"This is Rain. She's your sister. Aren't you going to say hello?"

18

"I wish it would *snow*," I said one winter, when there was nothing but hailstones and drizzle. Nana looked up from the scones she was baking. Her forehead was powdered with flour. She said, "Snow? No, thank you. Be careful what you wish for, Apple!" As though anything bad could come from snowmen and a bit of sledding down Cliff Gardens.

And another time I was brushing my hair, dragging out the knots and complaining. "I wish I had straight hair," I said. Nana looked up from her sewing and said, "Goodness me, what for? Be careful what you wish for, Apple!" As though anything bad could come from sleek locks.

And last spring, when it was raining outside and I was playing myself at Monopoly, I said, "I wish I had a sister." Nana held her cookie, undunked, over a teacup. She said,

"Oh, Apple, please, *please* be careful what you wish for."

As though anything bad could come from a ready-made friend.

All those times I was thinking that Nana was wrong, wrong, wrong.

But she was right.

I was the wrong, wrong, wrong one to wish for things I didn't have.

I should have been careful about my wishes.

And I should never have wished for a sister.

19

Rain is sitting on the couch, cradling a doll and shushing it. Mum is making coffee.

"So how old are you?" I ask Rain.

"Ten," Rain says. She kisses the doll's forehead. "And Jenny's six months." Rain holds the doll close. "I know you're hungry, sweetie pie. I'll get you milk in a minute."

I can't help staring. Rain isn't behaving like she's playing; she's acting like the doll is real.

Mum hands me a mug. "I don't know how you take it, so I gave you one sugar." She sounds anxious, as though not knowing how I take my coffee is her biggest concern. As though she hasn't got other things to explain.

"I've never had coffee before," I admit. It's the color of strong tea. I take a sip. It's bitter and thick—like clay. Mum sits on the floor under the window, blowing into her own coffee mug.

"Oh my goodness, is that smell what I think it is? Have you done a poop?" Rain laughs. "Come on, honey, let's change you." She leaves the room and shouts from the hallway in her nasal, American accent. "We gotta buy more diapers, *Mom*!"

Mum unbuttons her shirt at the wrists and rolls up her sleeves. "The doll is a phase. The doctor told me that she's completely normal," Mum says.

"Oh. Okay."

Mum lights a fresh cigarette. "It's best if you play along. No good upsetting her by telling her Jenny isn't real."

"Okay," I say again. But Rain's doll isn't the thing that's knocked me sideways. "When you said you had a big surprise for me, I thought maybe you had a boyfriend or something," I tell Mum.

"Boyfriend? No, I prefer to keep the men moving through." She laughs, alternating between the coffee and the cigarette.

"It's just that once Dad got Trish . . ."

But I don't have to finish the sentence. I see in Mum's eyes that she understands. "He changed," she says. "I could see it when I met him. So full of his own importance. And uptight. *Very* uptight."

Rain returns, patting her doll. "She's so tearful all the time. She can tell she's not at home," she says.

"I'm sure she'll feel better soon," Mum says.

"She needs a crib, Mom. She's getting too big to sleep with me."

Mum closes her eyes. "Let's look in Mothercare next week," she says, as though what Rain's asking for isn't beyond weird. As though there's space in our tiny bedroom for a cot. "We have to go shopping for your new school uniform anyway." Mum leans her head against the rusting radiator. "I'm so fricking tired," she says.

"What school are you going to?" I ask Rain.

Mum opens her eyes and grins. "She's going to Littleton Park Primary. And as it's right around the corner from your school, I thought you could walk together sometimes."

"I'm bringing Jenny to school with me," Rain says.

I don't want to walk with Rain, but Mum looks so happy about the idea, I can't say no.

"Sounds fun," I say, and put my mug to my mouth so I can bite on the rim.

*　　*　　*

We order pizza for dinner. With cans of lemonade and

garlic bread on the side. Afterward, Mum takes me into my bedroom and tells me to put my things in the plastic boxes she's hidden beneath the bunk beds. She hasn't had a chance to buy any wardrobes yet. "We'll get some soon," she says.

Rain is standing in the door frame. She kisses the doll's nose.

"Tomorrow evening I've arranged for some old friends of mine to come over to meet you both, so try to get a good night's sleep," Mum says.

"A party?" Rain whines. "Jenny hates them."

"It's not a party. It's . . ." Mum fondles the air for the right word, ". . . a do."

"A *do*? Like a doo-doo? Like poop?" Rain says.

"No, honey, you were right the first time. It'll be a small party," Mum says.

Rain stamps a foot.

"Let's have an early night so we can get up fresh and plan the food," Mum says. She takes our hands. "Both my babies with me again. What a day. Oh, what a day!" Her eyes water at the corners. "Good night then."

"Good night," I say. I watch her leave the room.

"I sleep up here with Jenny," Rain says. She climbs the

ladder to the top bunk. I ignore her and unzip my suit-case. "Don't use any of my boxes!" she shouts.

*   *   *

At three o'clock in the morning I give up trying to sleep. It's useless with Rain climbing in and out of her bunk—going back and forth to the kitchen every hour. I throw my legs over the side of the bed. "What are you *doing*?" I ask.

"Jenny's hungry at night." She waves a baby bottle of milk in my face.

Rain kneels on the floor with the doll lying in front of her and changes her diaper. Then she paces the room for ages humming "Twinkle, Twinkle, Little Star" into Jenny's plastic ear. The doll's eyes are fixed open.

"Can't you bring the baby to bed now?" I ask as kindly as possible even though I don't want to take this ridicu-lous game seriously.

Rain's eyes are white marbles in the dark. "Go home if you don't like it. This was *our* room before *you* came along."

Even in my half-asleep haze I feel hurt. Not because Rain doesn't want me around—that I get—but because it dawns on me that even though I see Rain as someone who's come along and spoiled things between me and Mum, really it's me who's new and out of place.

I burrow back beneath the covers and pull them up to my chin thinking about my bed at Nana's house, and how it was mine alone and no one else's. It would be nice to crawl into it. Just for a couple of hours.

20

Mum leaves me at home with Rain and goes to the supermarket where she buys baguettes, crackers, cheese, grapes, sweets, cookies, and bottles of wine and beer and Coke for the party, plus other groceries for the week. As I'm unpacking, I open a box of Jaffa Cakes for breakfast.

Rain rifles through the shopping I've piled along the counter. "You forgot Jenny's milk," she complains.

Mum pats Rain gently. "Look, here's the milk, honey."

"Two liters? That won't be enough for everyone," she says.

Mum sighs, and Rain goes storming off to the bedroom. She slams the door behind her so hard the walls shudder.

Mum shakes her head. "She throws away the old diapers and gets me to buy fresh ones. Now she's insisting on more and more milk. What next, a changing table?"

"I'll tell her the doll's not alive, if you like. I mean, I don't care if she gets mad at me," I say.

"I tried that six months ago when it all started. Don't think I didn't try. She pretends she can't hear you, or she'll act like you're making a joke. It hurts her to know the truth, and the doctor . . ." She trails off because she's already told me what the doctor said— it's a normal phase—but when will it end? Will she still be carrying it around when she begins secondary school—*my* secondary school? How long is everyone supposed to wait for her to figure it out? How long are we all supposed to pretend?

"Maybe you need a second opinion," I say quietly because all of a sudden Mum is rubbing her temples and breathing fast.

"I need to get her a therapist. She had a good one in Brooklyn but . . ." She looks at the shopping. "Maybe we should have stayed in America," Mum whispers.

"What?" If she'd stayed in America then where would that have left me?

"Oh, I don't mean it," she says. She blows me a kiss.

"I'll put away the food," I say.

"I'm not sure about the party anymore. Don't think

I'm in the mood," Mum says. Her forehead is furrowed with lines.

"But you bought all the stuff." I hold up a bunch of bananas, which makes her smile.

"Banana cocktails?" she asks.

"Sure! We'll mash them and mix them with this." I hold up what looks like a bottle of champagne.

"If people don't like the taste, we'll force-feed it to Jenny," Mum says. She laughs finally, but not before she sees Rain in the hallway, watching and clutching Jenny to her chest.

*   *   *

When I show Mum my neon-green T-shirt, she sucks in her cheeks. "For a party? Really?"

"I wore it to the school disco last term," I say. I feel my face flush because it's so obvious that Mum doesn't approve.

"How about something a little more . . . feminine," she says.

I'm not sure what she means. I don't wear skirts, except to school. I don't like showing off my legs.

"I've something that might fit you," she says, and dashes into her bedroom and out again, carrying a yellow dress. She holds it up to the window, so I can see it in the light. It's the same color as the one I wore when I was Trish's bridesmaid, but this dress has silver sequins along the neckline. "It'll look amazing."

"I'm not sure."

Mum presses the dress against me. "You can't go around in boys'clothes forever, you know, sweets." She winks, and I want to feel part of some lovely conspiracy, but I don't; I just feel really embarrassed.

So I go to the bathroom, put on the dress, and study my figure in the mirror. I don't feel like myself. I step into the hall.

"Wow!" Mum says.

"I look like I've been pumped full of custard," I say. I'm fatter than Mum, so the dress is tight across the stomach, but I have no breasts, so it sags at the chest.

Mum laughs loudly, throwing her head back and showing off her back teeth. "You look like a *girl*," she says. "Remind me what size shoe you take."

"Four," I mutter.

"I'm a five! And I've a lovely pair of sandals to go with that dress."

"Not high ones," I croak, but it's too late. She's in and out of her bedroom again and holding a pair of strappy high heels.

"I won't be able to walk in them," I say.

Mum kneels in front of me and slips the shoes on to my feet.

"Aren't sandals for the summer?" I say.

"Who cares? You can paint your toenails," she says, like that might keep my feet warm.

I try staggering around for a minute when Rain appears again.

"You look weird," she says. Her voice is flat and honest.

"She looks great!" Mum says, and puts her arm around me. I love the touch of that arm, especially facing Rain, and I feel myself expand.

The shoes suddenly feel less uncomfortable. The dress isn't so bad.

I go to the kitchen to arrange the snacks.

21

The party starts at eight, but no one shows up until ten when everyone piles through the door together. I carry around a plate of cheese and crackers, telling everyone I meet that I'm Mum's daughter.

"Annie's kid? Really?" "You look like her." "She really does!" "Cute dress!"

"Want some Brie?" I ask.

The food runs out quickly. The drinks don't. Everyone keeps sipping wine and the more they sip, the louder the room gets. Even though it's freezing out, the windows are open, so people can blow smoke through them. The music gets louder and louder.

"Apple, Apple, there's someone you have to meet," Mum shouts. She waves at me through the throng of people.

I weave my way toward her. She hands me her glass of

116

red wine. "You seem like you need a drink," she says. She laughs. The man next to her laughs too. And they're both watching me. I take a gulp of the wine. It tastes like cough medicine, only worse.

"This is Merlin," Mum says. She pushes the man toward me.

"As in the druid?" I ask.

The man nods like a mechanical toy. "Exactly. Although my real name's Martin. But who remembers a name like that?"

I take another swig of wine and shudder. Mum grabs a bottle of Coke from the kitchen counter and uses it to top off the glass.

I stare into the maroon concoction.

"Don't look so terrified. It's calimocho," she says.

Merlin sniffs. "Not without ice and lemon, it isn't. Ugh." He elbows past Mum and returns thirty seconds later with a fistful of ice, which he throws into my glass, splashing the drink all over my arm. Then he sticks a slice of lemon into it too.

I hope he has clean hands.

"Now *that's* calimocho," he says. "What do you think?"

I sip the cocktail, expecting it to taste no better, but it

is better. It's sweet with a little fizz. It's nice and cold. I can hardly taste the wine at all.

I smile.

"You don't have to be polite, you know. You can have plain old Coke," Mum says. She offers me an empty glass.

I shake my head. "It's good," I say.

Mum laughs. "A girl after my own heart. Now, Merlin, I have to tell you that Apple didn't want to wear the dress. But I told her she can't cover up her curves forever."

Merlin's eyes run up my legs to the dress and follow the lines of my body to my face. I want to tell him I'm only fourteen, but it might be rude to say something like that, so I go quiet instead. I hunch my shoulders to hide myself as much as I can. "She's a beauty, all right," he says. "Like her mother." Suddenly he pinches Mum's bum. I expect her to smack him. Instead, she laughs.

"Where's your other one?" Merlin asks.

"I don't know. Apple?"

How should I know where Rain is? She's probably tucked away somewhere trying to breastfeed.

"Can you make sure she's okay?" Mum asks.

For a second I don't move. But when Mum tilts her

head to the side and smiles, I just want to be useful. "Sure," I say. It's a small flat. She can't be far.

I find her curled up in the top bunk with Jenny. Her eyes are closed. She doesn't hear me come in. "Rain," I say. I touch her leg.

She jumps up and pulls out a pair of earphones. "What do *you* want?" She crawls into the corner where I can't reach her.

"Are you okay?"

"As if you care." She sits the doll on her lap and rests her chin on its head.

"Mum wants to know," I say.

"Well, you can tell *Mom* I'm fine, except Jenny can't sleep with all the noise. When are they leaving?"

I shrug. People are still arriving.

"But it's almost midnight," she says. She points to the clock above the tiny desk we'll have to share once she starts school.

"Why don't you come in and dance or something?"

"Is that booze?" she asks, staring at my glass.

"It's none of your business. Are you coming or not?" I ask. I know I'm not being nice. I can't help it.

Rain pulls the duvet over her head. "Get out!" she shouts.

*　*　*

Back in the sitting room, Mum is standing next to a woman with her hair wrapped in a multicolored scarf.

"Rain's okay," I say.

Mum blinks. "Huh? Oh yeah, good. Good."

"Who's this?" the woman asks.

"This is Apple, Gina," Mum says.

"Apollinia? No way. My God, I feel old," Gina says. She covers her eyes with her hands and screams.

"Gina was my best friend at school. She's been babysitting Rain for me," Mum says.

"We were *inseparable* until . . ." Gina trails off. She smiles at me awkwardly. I get it. They were friends until I came along and ruined everyone's fun. But I won't ruin anyone's fun now. I guzzle down the last of the calimocho in my glass.

"Can I get you a drink, Gina?" I ask.

Gina raises her eyebrows. "What have you got?"

"I'll make you a calimocho," I say.

"Sounds delicious," Gina says.

Mum laughs. "My girl," she says.

22

My head swims like I'm bobbing for apples. I sit up and open my eyes. I press my hand against my mouth to stop myself from being sick. The nausea passes. Slowly I sink into my pillow again and curl into a tight ball.

Rain comes into the room and bashes around under my bunk.

"What are you looking for?" I moan.

"Not my fault you're hungover," Rain says. She continues to rummage.

I rub my eyelids and try opening them again. I feel so sick I groan.

"You should've drunk water," Rain says.

"Thanks for the advice, but it's the middle of the night. Go back to sleep."

"It's six o'clock," she says. "Technically that's morning, and Mom says I can get up as long as it's after six. So go stick it."

"Please, Rain." I roll over.

She yanks a strange contraption from her box under the bed.

"What is that?" I ask.

"A carrier."

"What kind of carrier?"

"A baby carrier. I'm taking Jenny for a walk. Mom won't buy me a stroller."

My head sloshes. I go to the window and pull back the curtain. The street lamps are still on. The moon is glowing. "It's too dangerous to go out on your own. Wait until the sun comes up," I say.

"You're not my mother," she says. She snaps the carrier around her waist and stomps out. I listen to her getting ready and gaze outside at the wet road, the light from the yellow street lamps reflected in it.

I groan again and follow her into the sitting room.

Rain has the doll attached to her chest with the carrier and is pulling a coat over both of them.

"Watch TV until it gets light," I plead.

She ignores me.

"Fine, I'm coming with you." I put my coat on over my pajamas and slip my feet into Mum's knee-high boots. I look ridiculous. I feel even worse—like my head's a balloon that someone keeps trying to blow more air into.

We leave the house quietly and remain in silence all the way down to the seafront. The arcades and shops are still boarded up. The gulls are swooping back and forth across the beach looking for worms and bits of yesterday's sandwiches in the sand. The sun is rising. The sea has a grainy, orange tinge.

"I'm going for a swim," Rain says. She skips down the steps to the sand.

"It's freezing," I say.

"So what?"

I feel too sick to go with her, so I sit on a bench, looking at the waves nibbling the sand.

Rain takes off her sneakers and rolls up her jeans. She lets the freezing water cover her feet.

"Careful!" I shout.

She wades in until the water is up to her knees.

"Rain!"

I jump up and run to the shoreline. "You'll hurt Jenny!" I kick off Mum's boots. Rain turns. She blinks and walks toward me. Then she stands on the beach, looking down at her feet in the sand.

"I wasn't going to hurt her," she says.

"The sea is dangerous."

"Brooklyn is by the sea. I'm not stupid."

"Well, what if a massive wave pulled you in?"

"I come down here all the time." She finds a dry stretch of sand and sits so she can put her wet feet back into her sneakers. I do the same with the boots.

"What do you mean? At six in the morning when no one's around? It isn't safe. There could be . . . " I trail off. I want to say killers or pedophiles but that would make me sound like Nana—Nana's the last person I want to sound like.

"What could there be?"

"Gangs," I say.

"Gangs?"

"Gangs, yes."

Rain laughs, and it makes me stare at her teeth because I'm sure it's the first time I've seen them. "Brampton-on-Sea doesn't have gangs," she says.

All I can do is shrug.

On the promenade, a man is lifting up the metal shutters of his café.

"Morning," he says. He wipes down a chalkboard.

"Do you have any money?" I ask Rain.

She puts a hand into her jeans and pulls out a fiver.

"Want beans on toast?" I ask her. I don't know if I can stomach it, but if I don't eat something, I'm going to vomit all over Mum's boots.

"Ugh," Rain says. "What kind of beans?"

"Baked beans. Haven't you ever had beans on toast?"

She shakes her head.

"Welcome to England," I say. I grab the fiver and lead her inside.

*　　*　　*

When we get home, I sit on the couch next to Rain watching TV and eating chunks of cheese left over from the party. My head no longer hurts. But Mum looks awful—she has black rings under her eyes, her hair is knotted, and she's unusually pale.

"Hey," I say.

Mum goes to the kitchen where she reaches for a box of acetaminophen. She pops two into her mouth and washes them down with tap water.

"She's got a hangover like you," Rain says. She grabs the remote control from me.

"I think I must be coming down with something," Mum says. "And it's *not* a hangover, thank you very much, Rain."

Rain opens her mouth to respond when the doorbell jangles.

"Who the hell is that on a Sunday?" Mum complains. She ties her hair into a messy bun.

"Want me to go down?" I ask. I'm not dressed either, but I look better than she does.

"Yes. And whoever it is, tell them to skedaddle. Especially if it's Merlin. God, I couldn't get him to leave last night."

A memory of last night comes back to me: Mum talking to Merlin in the hall. They were standing very close to one another. I think they may have been holding hands.

I slip down the stairs and into the hall, expecting to see Merlin or Gina or someone else from last night, but when I open the door, Nana is standing there. Her face is screwed up, and she's holding her handbag against her body like she's scared someone's about to steal it.

"I was worried you might be sick," she says.

I shake my head. Could she know about the calimocho? "I'm okay. Why?"

"I need to see your mother."

I glance behind me. "Mum's not well."

Nana's eyes grow wide. "I'm coming in. I've a right to

know where you live," she says. She pushes past me up the stairs.

By the time I get into the sitting room, Nana and Mum are facing each other like animals about to attack.

"Why wasn't Apple at Mass today? Is she not going anymore? Is that a decision you've made for her?"

Mum tightens the belt on her dressing gown and folds her arms across her chest. "I forgot," Mum says.

And so had I. "Sorry, Nana. I'll come next week."

"Maybe if you were up before noon, it would help," Nana says to Mum. She scans the apartment, taking in the bottles, glasses, and paper plates from yesterday's party. "It stinks of alcohol and cigarettes in here. Is this the kind of life you're giving your daughter?"

"I'm sorry it isn't wholesome enough for you," Mum says.

Nana suddenly goes quiet. Without looking, I know what she's seen.

Rain is standing with Jenny in her arms staring at Nana.

The room is silent.

Nana lays her handbag on one of the cardboard boxes. "Are you one of Apple's friends?" she says quietly.

Rain shakes her head.

"No. No, I didn't think you were. What's your name?"

Rain looks at Mum. I think she might cry.

"This is your granddaughter. Her name's Rain," Mum says. Her voice is full of accusation, but I'm not sure what Nana's done wrong.

"Rain?" Nana whispers. She doesn't look angry anymore. She holds out her hand and beckons Rain toward her as though Rain's a shy puppy. I'd been so busy thinking about myself and the shock of having a new sister, I never thought about what it would be like for Nana to have another grandchild.

Rain stands like a statue.

Mum sighs. "This is your grandmother, Rain. I told you about her. I showed you a photograph, remember. This is her."

"Apple was living with you before, wasn't she?" Rain says.

Nana nods. "Yes, she was."

"Well, you can have her back if you like because we don't have room here," Rain says.

"Rain!" Mum shouts.

On films and TV I've seen reunions. Long-lost relatives hug and scream and cry. But this is nothing like that. This is the exact opposite of that. I don't want to be here—I want to go into my room and squeeze myself into one of the plastic boxes under the bed.

Nana looks at her hands and fiddles with her wedding ring. Then she turns to Mum with fire in her eyes. "How *dare* you?" she says.

"How dare I what?" Mum says. She clicks on the kettle she bought at the supermarket.

"Apple, please give us a minute," Nana says.

I wait for a sign from Mum, so I know whether to leave or not, but Mum is busy making herself a coffee.

"Please, Apple," Nana says.

I pull Rain down the hall into our room. We can still hear everything. We sit on my bunk listening, Rain clutching Jenny tighter than ever.

Nana: You didn't think to tell me you had another child?

Mum: Don't you come into my home ranting and raving.

Nana: I'll do what I like when my granddaughters are at stake.

Mum: They aren't your problem.

Nana: But why would you keep something like this from me? And from Apple? I just don't understand it.

Mum: It was for the best.

Nana: The best? The *best*? Whose best exactly? My God, Annie, you are unbelievable. You show up out of the blue and carry Apple off without one thought for how I feel. What's her view of this long-lost sister? Have you asked her?

Mum: Oh, give it a rest. Anyone would think I'd killed someone the way you go on.

Nana: I really don't know what I did wrong to make you behave like you do, Annie.

Mum: Well, I guess you did something.

Rain's small fingers tickle my leg. She's crying big bubbly tears. I try to put an arm around her shoulder, but she stiffens. I hold her hand instead.

"It's okay," I say. "They argue like this sometimes."

"I don't like it," Rain says.

"No," I say. Neither do I. But that's what happens every time Mum and Nana are together.

"They don't love each other," Rain says.

I'm not sure that's true. "They love each other, but I don't think they like each other very much," I say.

Rain frowns. "That doesn't make sense."

"Do you love Mum?"

She bites her thumb.

"Doesn't she ever get on your nerves?"

"Like, *always*."

"It's a bit like that. I have this dog called Derry, who's really sweet. I love him like mad, but sometimes he pukes on the stairs or farts when we're eating, and then I could really kick him."

She smiles. "Do you actually kick him?"

"No! I love him too much to kick him."

And finally she laughs, just as Mum appears around the door. "Nana's heading off now, if you want to say good-bye, Apple," she says.

I go into the living room where Nana is standing, looking into the sink piled with dirty dishes.

"I worry," she says quietly.

"I'm fine, Nana," I say.

Nana yanks a woolen hat from her bag and pulls it over her forehead. "Maybe you and Rain would like to come for dinner soon," she says.

I hesitate.

"Your mother said it would be okay."

"Okay," I say.

"Well, I'll head off then. I've plenty of things to do."

I only left Nana a couple of days ago, but already I've

forgotten how to act around her. I stand staring at her, wringing my hands.

Nana waits a couple of seconds, and when she realizes we're done, turns and heads down the stairs. "God bless you all," she calls out and leaves me feeling like a piece of me has left too.

PART 3
war

23

"Are you sure you want to take Jenny with you?" Mum asks Rain on our way to school. "I'd be happy to keep her with me."

"She'd cry," Rain says. She's sitting in the back of the car wearing the same green uniform I wore when I was at Littleton Park. Jenny is perched on her lap; Rain hasn't insisted on a car seat yet.

"Are you nervous?" I ask.

"I hope Jenny will be okay," she says.

Mum gives me a sideways look that says she doesn't believe Rain and pulls up next to my school gates. "Want a lift home?"

"I get a choice?" I ask.

"Huh?" Mum doesn't understand because she doesn't go around assuming murderers are after me.

"I'll walk," I say.

I open the car door and see Egan Winters locking up his bike. I brush my skirt with my hand.

"Who's that?" Mum asks.

"No one," I say. Heat rushes up my chest to my neck.

"What's his name?"

"Egan," I say.

"Egan? He's cute."

"Who's cute?" Rain asks, suddenly interested.

"Why don't you ask him out?" Mum says.

She must be crazy. I shake my head. "He's a senior."

"So? If you like him, what does it matter? You have to get him," Mum says. She ruffles my hair and loosens my tie.

"You're making her look like a homeless person," Rain says.

"Shut up," I say.

Mum leans in with a stick of gloss. She smears it across my lips. "It's a start," she says. "Now go on."

I climb out of the car and walk through the school gates. Mum drives off without beeping or waving or doing anything else remotely embarrassing.

I reach the main doors at the same time as Egan Winters. I pause to let him through first.

"No, go on," he says.

Is he speaking to me? I look up, stunned. Egan Winters has a bike chain slung over his shoulder. And he is peering at me.

"Thanks," I say. I try smiling, but it's so strained I probably look like I'm choking on a marble.

Not that Egan Winters notices. His phone rings and he answers it. "Mate!" he says. "No way. Mate, *no way.* You're such a mug." He laughs and pushes past me into the school.

* * *

The rest of the day goes as I expected. I'm alone in lessons, at lunch, and in the corridors walking between classes. I hum whenever I see Donna or Pilar so they'll think I don't care that they're best friends now. I keep my back straight and paste a smile across my face. They choose Hazel and Mariah for their group in English, and I sit by the wall alone. I use charcoal on paper to draw the images I find in the war poems Mr. Gaydon has given us. I try to concentrate really hard on the work.

My favorite poem is by someone called Rupert Brooke. He makes war sound brave and beautiful and all the people who fight in it like heroes. When Mr. Gaydon looks at my drawings, I tell him this. He answers me using a really loud voice that is meant for everyone else in the class to hear. "Ah, yes, you're right, Apple. 'The Soldier' by Rupert Brooke is rather patriotic." He lifts his chin and quotes from the poem:

> *"If I should die, think only this of me;*
> *That there's some corner of a foreign field*
> *That is for ever England."*

"Sounds magnificent. But Rupert Brooke might not have written that if he'd known he was about to die himself. Look at this."

Mr. Gaydon goes to the Smartboard. He opens the Internet and displays a picture of a man with spongy hair. "That's Rupert Brooke. He died during the war when he was twenty-seven. He was in France on an expedition. Do you know how he died?" We all sit there. How would any of us know? "Mosquito bite," Mr. Gaydon says.

Some kids laugh. Mr. Gaydon doesn't. "Not exactly the glorious death he imagined. And I doubt any death on the battlefield is as romantic or heroic as poems or films or anything else would make it seem. The poetry from the First World War is particularly sad because by the end, no one quite remembered why they were fighting." Mr. Gaydon pauses, waiting for someone to say something clever. All I can think about is myself; how I get hot and angry with people and then a few days later I'm still mad, but I'm not sure why anymore.

"He's cute," Sharon Bowerman says from the front of the room.

Mr. Gaydon rolls his eyes. "Thank you, Sharon. He isn't cute though. He's dead. That's what war does. It kills people. Nothing else. It hurts the innocent and guilty alike because it doesn't discriminate."

I stop listening and focus on Donna. She is holding her chin in her hand. She is staring at Mr. Gaydon with a thin smile. Her dad is in the army. He's away at war now, and Donna always acts like he's a big hero. But Mr. Gaydon's kind of saying that war is pointless, and the more he goes on, the thinner Donna's smile gets.

"So your homework is to write about *your* war. Who are you at war with and why? Could be your parents or your teachers or maybe your own addiction to almonds." He laughs. No one else does. Mr. Gaydon is nice, but he isn't funny. "Think about Wilfred Owen's poetry when you're writing. And Sassoon's."

"I'll definitely be thinking about Rupert Brooke," Sharon shouts out.

"I'm sure you will, Sharon," Mr. Gaydon says. And the last bell rings.

*　　*　　*

I'm lumbering through the playground wishing I'd told Mum to pick me up, and as if she's read my mind, there she is. But unlike Nana who'd be practically holding up a sign with my name on it, Mum is at the railings wearing a black leather jacket and sunglasses. She doesn't stick out at all. Actually, she looks cool.

"I hope you don't mind me showing up. The car was hissing at me so I dropped it off at the garage. I was walking this way anyway to collect Rain. I'll slink off, if you want."

"No, no." I kiss her cheek proudly. "I'm happy you're here."

"And look who else is here," Mum says. She tilts her head and winks.

Egan Winters is unlocking his bike. He must sense us watching him and looks up. The sun is in his face. He squints.

"Come with me," Mum says. She starts toward him.

"*Mum*," I say under my breath. It's too late. She's gone. I shuffle after her.

"Hey, how's it goin'?" she says to Egan. She sounds more American than usual.

"Fine," he says. He hangs his bag across the bike frame.

Mum touches the reflector near the handlebars. "I'm gonna buy Apple a bike. How do you like this one?" she says. If Nana were talking to him, I'd die on the spot, but Mum's different. She's young and pretty and dresses a bit like a senior.

Egan sniffs. "It's okay."

"Not like having a car, right?"

"My uncle's a mechanic, so he'll set me up with a car when I pass my test. I'm taking it soon," Egan says.

"Let me guess: a Ford Fiesta?" She tucks her hair behind her ears.

Egan smiles. "Nah. I want a BMW. Metallic black. Leather interior."

"Dream on," Mum says.

Egan laughs. "Exactly!"

Mum puts her arm around me. "Do you know my daughter?"

Egan looks at me—like, really and truly looks at me. "You play the oboe, don't you? What year you in?"

141

"Uh, eighth grade. I play the clarinet."

"You play an instrument too?" Mum asks.

"In school I play the flute. My dad's a music teacher. I also play bass guitar. I'm in a band called The Farewells."

"Nice," Mum says. "And what's your name?"

"Egan," he says.

"Well, good to meet you. We'd better go. See you around, Egan," Mum says.

"Bye," I say.

Egan throws one leg over his bike.

When I catch up with Mum, she pinches my elbow. "Next time we'll invite him to the party."

"What party?"

"Oh, for goodness' sake, Apple, the Egan Winters party," she squeaks. "I can hardly wait."

* * *

Rain is sitting on the curb outside Littleton Park Primary holding Jenny. Her red curls are loose and tangled. The knees of her white tights are gray. She has the beginnings of a black eye.

Mum sits next to her. "Where are your glasses?"

"In my bag. They broke," Rain says.

"How?"

"Everyone in England is stupid, that's how. They tried to take Jenny away when we were having PE, and then some of the kids said dumb things. So I hit them. I gave a boy a bloody nose."

Mum picks at her lips. "You started a fight? Oh, Rain, *why*?"

"I told you. They were *mean*. I'm not coming back here."

"We'll talk about that later, but first I want to speak to them myself. I'm going inside for a minute. You wait with Apple."

"Whatever," Rain says.

Mum pulls at the cuffs of her leather jacket and marches into the school.

I sit next to Rain on the curb. "You have to go to school. Jenny will be fine with Mum at home."

"Would *you* leave your baby with her?" Rain asks.

I pick up a gray stone and roll it between my fingers. "Probably." I think about myself as a baby and how much I needed Mum. How I've always needed her.

"Then you don't know her very well," Rain says. She stands and heads up the hill.

"Where are you going?" I call out.

"Home," she says. "These meetings always take forever."

"You've had fights at school before?"

"Loads of times. I broke a girl's finger once."

I chase after her. "You what?"

"It was only her little finger." She touches her bruised eye.

Anyone would think from the look and sound of Rain that she's tough. But for some reason, I can't help wanting to protect her.

24

Light filters through the curtains. I bolt upright and grab my phone. It's nine thirty. "Damn," I say aloud and jump out of bed. I've never slept in before. I've never been late for school.

The bunk above creaks. "What's wrong?" Rain asks.

"Uhh." I rub my head. I didn't mean to have anything to drink last night, but Gina and Merlin came over for dinner and Mum made martini cocktails. I couldn't resist tasting one.

"You hungover *again*?" Rain asks.

"Don't be stupid. I'm late. And so are you. Get a move on." I don't have time for a shower. I hardly have time to brush my hair. I pull on my gray uniform and grab my schoolbag from under the desk. My English exercise book falls out and lies open in front of me accusingly. I tut.

"Now what?" Rain hasn't moved.

"I forgot about my homework."

"Me too," she admits. "But I'm not going in anyway. Mum said I could stay home."

"She what?"

Rain climbs down the ladder with Jenny. "She said all the teachers are loony tunes."

"Which ones?" The teachers I knew at Littleton Park were all really nice. They read us stories and sang with us. Sometimes they gave us fun-sized Snickers. I don't remember any of them being crazy.

"*All* of them are loons," Rain says. She picks up the spotty socks she wore yesterday and puts them on.

"I'm going to get some breakfast," I say.

Mum is in the kitchen wearing a cream blouse and skinny jeans. "Morning, honey," she says. She blows me a kiss.

"Why didn't you wake me?" I ask.

"I did put my head around the door and shout, but you were out cold. Late night, last night. Anyway I've a meeting in half an hour with an agent. She gets everyone a part in *EastEnders*. Apparently."

"*EastEnders* from the telly?"

"Can you believe it?"

I can't. If Mum was an actress on *EastEnders*, she'd be famous. I'd have a famous mum. And Nana couldn't stop me watching it.

"Right, some coffee and I'm gone," Mum says. "Do you need me to write you a note to explain why you're so late? I'll say you were at the dentist. Isn't Rain up yet?"

"She said she doesn't have to go to school."

Mum bites into her toast. Crumbs fall to the floor. She looks down and sweeps them to the side with her foot. "I'll send her back when all this Jenny business is over with. The kids are giving her a hard time, and the teachers aren't much better. I'll let her hang around with me for a bit."

"What if she never realizes that Jenny is a doll?"

Mum frowns. "I hadn't thought that far ahead," she says.

She stamps the pedal on the bin and throws the toast into it. She grabs a blunt green pencil. "Get me a piece of paper to write the note," she says.

I don't move. I really wish I didn't have to go in. I haven't got any friends. Plus, I didn't do my homework. I don't want Mr. Gaydon to think I don't care—since he showed up, English is my favorite class. I actually like writing poems.

Rain stumbles into the kitchen in her nightie. "Why aren't you *ready*?" Mum says. She tries to shoo Rain back down the hall. "I can't be late. I want this agent to take me on. And we need the money from a steady gig."

"Stop pushing me," Rain whines.

"You're being purposefully difficult. You can have a KitKat to take on the bus if you're hungry. Just *get dressed*."

Rain stamps her foot in a temper.

Mum looks at her watch.

"Why are you taking the bus? Haven't you got your car back from the garage yet?" I ask.

"Huh?" Mum scratches her neck and slips her feet into a pair of high shoes.

Rain slides past her into the kitchen, opens the fridge, and pours milk into a baby bottle.

"Rain, what the hell are you *doing*?" Mum says. She rubs her temples.

"Jenny has to eat, in case you'd forgotten," Rain says.

Mum checks her watch again and puts her hand on my shoulder. "Apple, I know this is a big thing to ask, but can you watch Rain for me? I'll be home before five. Can you do that?"

"I don't need a stupid babysitter. Not *her* anyway," Rain says.

"Apple?"

Mum doesn't have time to wait for me to deliberate. She rummages in her handbag and throws a tenner at me. "Get pizza for lunch," she says.

"I'm sick of pizza," Rain says.

Mum lowers her voice. "And I'm sick of . . ." She pauses. Rain stares at her. "I'm sick of . . . I'm sick of always being late," she says. She grabs her coat from the hall stand, bangs down the stairs, and slams the front door behind her.

"Good riddance!" Rain shouts.

I fall onto the couch. I don't want to go to school, but keeping Rain in line isn't my idea of a day off.

"You don't have to look so miserable," Rain tells me.

"Leave me alone. I'm going to do my homework," I say. "And if you plan to stay home for a while, maybe you should read some books."

"I haven't got any books," she says.

"You haven't got any books?"

She shakes her head. I'm stunned.

So we go to the library.

25

In the children's section of the library, a squadron of toddlers are banging spoons,\blowing whistles, and screaming along to nursery rhymes. I want to leave, but Rain says Jenny might like the rhymes. She sits in the circle with the doll on her lap. Some of the mothers throw her suspicious looks. The singing librarian gives Rain a wide, welcoming wave. After a couple of songs, Rain joins in with the singing. I leave her to it and flop down in front of a computer in the research section.

A librarian with spiky white hair points at a sign above my computer: 30 MIN LIMIT FOR PCS.

"If you're doing some homework, you don't have to worry about that. We just don't want people sitting here and spending five hours chatting online. Do you know how to work the computer?" She looks about Nana's age and even has a bit of Nana's soft lilt.

"Yes, thank you," I say. I open a new document, expecting her to go back to her work. She stands with one hand on my desk, looking at the screen.

"Is it a training day?" she asks.

"Huh?"

"You're not at school. Is it a staff training day?"

"Uh, yeah," I say. "The teachers have a meeting."

"And they'll be on strike next month. What do they expect parents to do with their kids all day?"

I lightly tap the keyboard without writing anything.

"Well, if you need help, I'm over there," she says, and walks away.

I type slowly and check over my shoulder occasionally to make sure no one is reading what I'm writing.

"War" by Apple Apostolopoulou

It doesn't look like war
Unless you examine it closely—with your glasses on,
Drawing your finger over the cracks in the friendship.
We were a pair,
A team of two
Until Donna took her
Away—

Swooped down and grabbed Pilar
Like an eagle diving for fish at the edge of the ocean.
I never thought that could happen.
I thought for ever friends meant just that:
For ever and for ever and for ever.
Now I know it means
Until.
Until someone better comes along,
Until the conductor swipes her baton,
Chooses you, not me, and
Ends our symphony.

I get to one hundred words then turn to check on Rain. She is fully engrossed in a wild rendition of "Head, Shoulders, Knees, and Toes." Jenny has lost a shoe.

I read through what I've written, but as usual, it's too close to the truth. I can't hand it in.

I open a fresh document and start again:

"War" by Apple Apostolopoulou

I don't understand people who make football into
war. My dad loves Arsenal. He's their biggest fan, but
I don't think he really likes watching them play all

that much because when he does, he gets really angry.
He shouts and swears and knocks the stuffing from
cushions. And he acts as though the players on the
other team are evil. He tells me he hates the managers
of the other teams too. In England there are a lot of
football hooligans who go to games just to have
fights. But football is a sport, so it should be fun.

"How do I print?" I call over to the librarian.

She smiles. "I'll print it for you," she says. She comes
and sits on the chair next to mine. I don't want her reading
what I've written, but she doesn't. She presses some buttons and gets the printer set up. Across the room, it gurgles
to life.

She jumps up and returns with my English homework.

I fold the paper and put it into my bag. "Thank you,"
I say.

She bows slightly as Rain comes bounding over from
the children's section. "Jenny *really* loved that!" she says.
Her face is flushed from dancing and singing.

"It was nice of you to bring her along," I say. I'm being
sort of sarcastic, but Rain doesn't notice. "Okay, shall we
get books so you have something to do at home for the
rest of the week?" I ask.

The librarian frowns and looks like she's about to ask a question. I quickly pull Rain by the arm back into the children's section.

"Right, you need some fiction and nonfiction. I think if you get one history, one science, and two novels, that'll be enough for today."

Rain looks around at the shelves. "Can I take them home?"

"It's a library, Rain, of course you can. Haven't you ever borrowed a book from a library?"

"Nope. I read stuff on Mum's iPad."

"But . . ." I look along the shelves. I never choose a book without picking it up and flicking through the pages. I always read the first few lines. "Come on, I'll show you the ones I like," I say. I take her to the fiction section, and we explore.

Rain is sitting on the floor with her legs crossed, completely engrossed in a mystery about a girl who goes to sleep one night in her parents' boring old house in Croydon and wakes up the next day in a Victorian London orphanage. I'm reading the brand-new Mallary Ford novel, which I've been waiting for ages for the library to get in. I've also found a book of poems by someone called Emily Dickinson. Most of them are short. I scan my eye over one or two and decide to give the collection a try.

"Shall we get these then?" I say. I pat the pile of books we've chosen.

Rain doesn't look up from her reading.

"Let's get going." I pull her to her feet.

We're on our way to the front desk when I see Nana chatting with the white-haired librarian. I yank Rain behind a bookcase.

"Ouch. Don't hurt me."

"Shh." I press my index finger to my lips. "Nana's here. If she sees us . . ." I stop because I don't know what she'd do. All I know is that I don't want to find out.

"She's not *my* nana," Rain says.

"Yes, she is. Or your nan or gran or grandma or whatever you want to call her," I whisper.

Rain peers around the bookcase. "Is she nice?"

"Yes. She's . . . very nice." I take a peek myself, using one eye.

Nana is leaning on the circulation desk, watching the librarian scan the bar codes. She isn't crying or frowning or anything like that, but she looks sad. Her eyes look sad. And her shoulders are rounded.

I hide behind the bookcase again.

"Is she okay?" Rain asks, seeing it too.

"Don't know. Maybe Derry's sick or Nana fell out with someone at the church," I say. But if it is one of those things, then why do I feel so guilty? I sneak another look as Nana drops her books into her shopping cart and slowly shuffles out of the library. I've always thought of Nana as old-fashioned, but I never thought she was *old*. Not until now, and it makes me want to chase after her.

"What's happening?" Rain asks.

"Nothing," I say.

I take her to the desk to have our books checked out.

"You're lucky to snap this one up," the librarian says. She holds up the Mallary Ford novel.

"I know. I love her books," I say quietly.

I don't sound excited—I can't be. All I can think about are Nana's sad eyes and rounded shoulders. All I can think about is how I probably should have helped her wheel home the shopping cart.

26

Even though Mum's not home at five o'clock like she said she would be, I don't worry. I don't even worry at six o'clock. Instead, I put a frozen cottage pie into the oven and set the dining table for when she does get home. I fold the paper napkins in two and arrange them smartly in the glasses like they do at restaurants. I put a bottle of white wine in the fridge.

At seven o'clock she still isn't home. When I call her cell phone, she doesn't answer.

"Where is she?" Rain asks, even though she *knows* I don't know. I feel like telling her to shut up, but I don't. It isn't her fault Mum's late.

"Have you got any of her friends' phone numbers?" I ask.

"Do you think something bad has happened to her?"

"Don't be stupid," I say. But my belly's becoming a ball

of dough that feels like it's rolling around inside me—heavy and raw. "Why don't you give Jenny a bath? I'm sure Mum'll be back before bedtime," I say. I try to sound convinced.

I distract myself from thinking about Mum being hurt by cleaning the kitchen. I shine the taps and the stove and the fronts of all the cupboards. I empty the crumbs out of the toaster.

I'm on my knees under the table with the dustpan and broom when Rain comes back in. Jenny is wrapped in a towel. Rain looks in the fridge, then slams it.

"We've no milk, and Jenny's hungry," she says.

I look up and bump my head on the corner of one of the chairs. "Jenny's fine. Give her some water," I snap. I rub my head.

"She won't sleep without milk."

"Rain, come *on*. It's dark and drizzly outside, and Mum's still not home."

"Fine. I'll go get it myself." She puts a hat on Jenny and clambers into her jacket.

"Get back here." I crawl out from under the table and catch hold of her hood.

"Hey!" She screeches much louder than she needs to. "You jerked my neck. And you've upset the baby."

I feel my eyes well with tears. I press my knuckles against my lids and take a deep breath. "Jenny will catch a chill. *I'll* get the milk," I say.

"You have to say sorry for hurting me, or I'll tell Mom."

"Tell her whatever you like," I say.

I run all the way to the corner shop at the bottom of our road. It smells of raw chicken and dust. The fridges are almost empty. The only milk they have is a really big carton of skim. I dig in my pocket and pull out the money left from the tenner Mum gave me this morning—ninety-five pence—not nearly enough. "Excuse me," I say to the woman who is stacking shelves with boxes of dishwasher tablets behind me.

"What?"

"I need a small milk."

"If it's not out, we haven't got it."

"I don't have enough money for a big one."

"And?" She clicks her tongue.

"I need to feed a baby," I say.

A man in a gray suit reaches over me and picks up two fruit yogurts. I wonder if I could ask him for a pound, but I don't want him to think I'm a beggar.

I leave the shop and stand outside. I won't go home

empty-handed. I can't handle Rain when she has a melt-down. The dough ball in my belly starts to swell, and I think I might scream into the sky. Jenny isn't even real, but I'm standing outside some smelly shop in the dark wondering how I can feed her real food.

And maybe that's my own problem. Because she doesn't actually need real food. We could feed her sea-water mixed with chalk dust and she'd be okay. There's no reason for me to be embroiled in Rain's fantasy.

So I go back into the shop and buy a small bag of plain flour which costs ninety-five pence exactly.

* * *

I sneak into the flat and mix the flour with water, shaking it up in one of Jenny's bottles. Then I tip the rest of the flour into an empty, airtight tub for cereal and pop it into the cupboard. "Rain!" I call to her.

She comes out wearing a Mickey Mouse T-shirt and Christmas tights with snowmen down the sides. Jenny is dressed in a onesie. "What took you so long?" she says. Her eyes and nose are all red. She must have been crying. Her breathing is quick and light.

"Mum called my cell when I was out. She'll be home soon," I lie. I shake the baby bottle again and hand it to her. "Here. They didn't have any milk, so I got formula."

Rain takes the bottle and looks at it suspiciously. "What kind of formula?"

"Uh . . . I can't remember the brand. Mix one table-spoon with water. It's better for the baby than milk. Has all the vitamins and things she needs."

"Okay," she says. She pretend-feeds Jenny the concoction and tries a smile with the corner of her mouth but bites it away as the noise of keys rattling and a door opening trickles up the stairs. Rain grimaces like she has a bad taste in her mouth. "About time," she says. Without waiting to make sure Mum's okay, she heads back down the hall and closes our bedroom door.

Mum comes bundling up the stairs, carrying an armful of papers and mail and holding her house keys in her mouth. I take the keys from her, and she puts the papers on the kitchen counter. "Oh, Apple, you couldn't put the kettle on for me, could you? I've had the worst day imaginable."

"Sure!" I fill the kettle and pop a spoon of instant coffee into a mug for her. Then I remember we've no milk. "You'll have to have it black," I tell her.

She flops on to the couch without noticing how clean the flat looks. "I'll have anything. Such a lousy day."

"Why?"

"You don't want to know."

"Did the agent say she could get you a part on *EastEnders*?"

Mum reaches into her handbag for her cigarettes. She lights one and sighs. "No. The agent was a scam artist. I ended up going into London to meet an old tutor of mine about getting some backstage work, but when I took him to dinner, he made a pass at me. He thought it was a date. A date? The guy's, like, sixty."

"So you didn't get a part in anything?"

"Zilch. I'll have to make appointments to see the agents in London. I need my name out there. But God, the trains are expensive."

"What about your car?"

"I can't afford it right now. It was only a hire car anyway."

"Oh," I say.

She looks up sharply. "What is it?"

"Nothing," I say quickly. I'm probably tired from looking after Rain and worrying about Nana and Mum. "I tried to call you."

Mum shows me her cell. "Dead battery."

"Okay."

"You aren't annoyed with me, are you, Apple?"

"No. It's just that Rain was upset you weren't home on time," I say. I hand Mum a cup of steaming coffee. She inhales the steam coming from it and smiles.

"Lovely." She stubs out her cigarette on the clean saucer and taps the cushion next to her. I cuddle in close. "If Rain hadn't been so slow this morning, she could have come with me. To be honest, Apple, I'm getting a bit tired of it all. Since this business with Jenny, I've hardly had a second to myself. She was bullied in New York and now she's being bullied here. Am I supposed to give up my dreams and take care of her? She's not a baby. It's so *hard*, Apple." She pulls me tighter into her. "Thank you for taking charge today. It really put my mind at ease. I'm so glad you're here to help."

"Me too," I say.

Mum drains her mug of coffee and plonks it on the side table. "I'm starved. I hardly ate anything at dinner," she says.

I jump up and skip to the kitchen. "We have cottage pie," I say.

"You know what I fancy? Some cheese on toast," Mum

says. She blows me a kiss. "And I think I'll have a glass of wine with it."

I take the wine from the fridge.

"I'm going to save a fortune on cleaners, cooks, and nannies," Mum says. She laughs.

I pour her a big serving of white wine, and the glass sweats. I hand it to her, and she takes a long gulp. "Delicious. Now pass the bottle over here. I don't want to make you keep refilling it."

"I don't mind," I say. And I don't.

"You're one of a kind, Apollinia Apostolopoulou, you know that?"

Living with Nana and having a strange name has always made me feel abnormal. But when Mum says I'm one of a kind, she only means it in a good way.

I throw away the cottage pie and turn on the grill to make her cheese on toast.

It's going to be the best cheese on toast ever.

PART 4
love

27

I forget to bring an absence note with me to school the next day, and Mrs. Wilkins, my homeroom teacher, acts as though I've committed a violent crime. "Everyone else manages to remember their sick notes, Apple. Please don't forget it tomorrow," she says.

"Yes, miss," I say.

"*Yes, miss,*" Donna mocks from across the classroom.

A few other girls giggle. But instead of sinking in my seat, which I would usually do, I give Donna the finger. I've never given *anyone* the finger before.

"Miss, Apple just swore at me," Donna calls out.

"Apple? Did you swear?" Mrs. Wilkins asks.

"I didn't say anything."

Mrs. Wilkins comes to my desk. "I'll speak to you after registration." Behind her, Donna is smirking and then she gives me the finger back and the whole class laughs. I don't bother telling Mrs. Wilkins. What's the point?

The bell rings, and Mrs. Wilkins dismisses the class. I stay where I am, and as Donna leaves, she scratches her middle finger along my desk. I try to catch Pilar's eye, to see if she's ready to be friends again, but she bundles out with everyone else and doesn't look at me.

Mrs. Wilkins is wiping the board. "Swearing is punishable by detention," she says. She raises her eyebrows.

"I know, miss," I say.

"Can you promise me you won't do it again? If you can, I'll pretend it didn't happen."

"Yes, miss," I say. I try to look really sorry. It's always the best tactic with Mrs. Wilkins.

"Fine," she says. "You can go."

But as I try to leave, Dr. Dillon, the assistant principal, rushes in.

"Ah, Mrs. Wilkins, I had hoped I'd catch your class before they left for lessons," Dr. Dillon says. She pushes her hand through her long gray hair, then slips it into the pocket of her blazer. She rocks back and forth in her patent leather shoes. She's so tall I can see right up her nose.

"I did wait until the bell rang, Doctor Dillon," Mrs. Wilkins says nervously.

"Yes, yes. That's all right. Only we have a new student today. I wanted to find a buddy for him. Is the group together for the next lesson?"

A boy is standing in the corridor, examining the science display on the wall. He isn't dressed in the correct uniform. He's got a gray shirt on underneath his sweater, not white, and he's wearing combat trousers instead of plain black ones, which no one except the eleventh graders ever tries to get away with.

"It's foreign languages," Mrs. Wilkins says. This means we're split into different groups; we won't be together again until English, which is after lunch.

Mrs. Wilkins sidles past Dr. Dillon and into the corridor. "Let me see your schedule," she says to the boy. He turns around and hands her the paper he's holding. And I recognize him immediately. He's the boy I met in Nana's garden—the one with the animal sweaters and war paint. Del.

Mrs. Wilkins runs her finger along Del's schedule. "Right, so you've got French now." She turns to me. "Apple, come here."

I inch my way out of the classroom.

"You have French now with Madame Moreau, don't you?"

169

I nod slowly. I know where this is all leading, but the last thing I need with Pilar ignoring me and Donna being mean is to be seen hanging around with the new boy. I rub my temples with the tips of my fingers.

Dr. Dillon appears next to me. She twitches and flattens down the lapels on her blazer. "What's wrong with you?" she asks. She takes my shoulders.

I groan. My head suddenly feels full of pressure.

"Do you need to see the nurse?" Mrs. Wilkins asks. I almost say yes because then I might get sent home, but it's a Tuesday, and orchestra is on Tuesday, which means I'll see Egan Winters. Now that Mum has spoken to him and he's spoken to me, he can't pretend I don't exist; he'll have to say hello.

"I've got a headache, miss," I say.

"Well, drink some water, dear," Dr. Dillon says. "I'm so late. Mrs. Wilkins, please find a home for this boy." She doesn't wait for Mrs. Wilkins to answer. She swivels around, her shoes squeaking on the floor, and sails off down the corridor.

Mrs. Wilkins smiles. "Right, Apple, to make up for your swearing, I'd like you to take care of our newcomer. Forget his schedule. Let him shadow you." She taps me on the head, turns around, and is gone as quickly as Dr. Dillon.

Del smiles. "Swearing? You never struck me as a rebel, Apple Blossom."

"Don't call me Apple Blossom," I snap.

He lifts up his hands in surrender. "How about Grapefruit Bloom? Can I call you Grapefruit?"

"You're not funny."

"I know. It's a curse. The worst thing about it is that my dad's a professional comedian."

"No, he isn't."

"No. He isn't. But wouldn't it be cool if he was?" Del isn't carrying a normal schoolbag. Instead, he's got a cream canvas tote over his shoulder. It's got pictures of cartoon mermaids on it, their long hair barely covering their breasts. If he thinks the other kids are going to let him get away with that, he's deluded. And if I let him use it, I'll be killed by association.

"Get rid of the bag," I say.

"How will I carry my . . ." He looks inside. "Pencils, cheese sandwich, and a flask of elderberry tea." He takes his sandwich from the bag, unwraps the brown paper, and takes a bite.

"It's nine o'clock in the morning," I tell him.

"So?" He takes another bite from his sandwich even though his mouth is still full. "I'm a growing boy. I'd eat a whole cow if Mum would let me. Or a dog. Did you know that they eat dogs in Korea? Like real dog. I wouldn't be totally against eating a dog." He laughs because he's joking, but it makes me think of Derry. I miss his stinky breath and golden hair. I miss snuggling with him and taking him for long walks down by the sea and even cleaning up his sick when he eats something he shouldn't. He ate a whole corn on the cob last summer when Dad was over and we were having a barbecue. Nana had to take him to the vet for an operation to remove it.

"Why didn't you bring a big beef burger, if you're so ravenous?" I ask.

"No meat at home. We're vegan. Well, Mum and Dad are."

"I hate to tell you this, but cheese isn't vegan," I say.

"Thanks for that precious info, Einstein. But actually, *this* cheese *is* vegan. The problem is that it tastes like condoms."

I can't help laughing, and then he laughs too.

"Not that I've ever eaten a condom. I've actually never even seen one in real life, but don't tell anyone that. I want all the girls here to think I'm 'Romeo, Romeo! wherefore art thou Romeo?'"

"Girls here don't like boys like Romeo."

"Who do they like?" he asks.

I imagine Egan Winters and smile.

"Why've you got that freaky look on your face? Is your headache really bad?" Del asks.

"Put your stuff in your pockets. You can't use the mermaid bag," I tell him. I take off down the corridor. "Now come on, Madame Moreau hates people being late!"

Del runs behind me. "Your nan was speaking to my mum. Told her you'd moved out. So you won't be back?"

"It's not really any of your business."

"Mum said your nan started crying. Mum says she misses you like mad."

I stop outside Madame Moreau's classroom. I'm panting from the run. I want to ask Del more about Nana. What exactly did she say to his mum? Why was she crying? For a second my throat feels like someone's stoppered it up with a cork. My head thrums.

Del holds me up. "You all right, Apple?" he asks.

I push him away. "Of course I am. I think my headache has turned into a migraine."

The classroom door opens, and Madame Moreau glowers at me. Behind her the room is dark and French voices blare from the Smartboard. "Why are you chatting in the hallway and not sitting at a desk, Mademoiselle

Apostolopoulou?" she asks. She's the only teacher who ever attempts to say my surname.

"I was showing the new boy around." I point stupidly at Del like the new boy could be anyone else.

"Go in and sit down," she says.

I slink into the classroom. Pilar is by the window on her own because Donna studies Italian. I consider sitting next to her, but if she wanted me to, she'd have waved me over. I take a seat at the back, and Del plops down next to me. He moves his chair closer.

"Hey, we're not friends, you know," I whisper.

"Yes, we are," he says. He leans forward and rests his head in his cupped hands.

I stare at the Smartboard. The French actors drone on and on. And even though I know Madame Moreau is going to make us answer questions about the film when it's over, I don't bother trying to understand anything.

* * *

After class I rush out of the door, followed by Del. I stand in the corridor next to a display of postcards written in French. Pilar eventually comes out of class. Now that she's alone, I might be able to get her to see what a cow Donna is. Maybe I could convince her that we should be friends again.

"Hey, Pilar," I say. I try to look nonchalant.

She stops and smiles. She adjusts the strap on her schoolbag. It's obvious she's uncomfortable and would prefer not to do this. Straightaway I regret trying to talk to her. It's pointless. She doesn't care one bit about me anymore. "What's going on?" she asks.

I shrug. I've so much to tell her about Mum, and Rain, and Nana, but I can't trust her with my secrets. Not now she's decided that Donna's the most glorious person on the planet. "Nothing you'd care about," I say. Not anymore.

Pilar doesn't try to coax me into telling her anything. She's too busy staring at Del. "Are you new?" she asks. Her voice is light and friendly. When Del turns around, he peers at her.

"This is Del. Doctor Dillon asked me to keep him company for the day."

"Cool," she says. She flicks her hair over her shoulder. It looks like she's straightened it. She bites her bottom lip. I think she might be flirting.

"We've got to go to math," I say. I don't want to be Del's best friend, but if Pilar wants a boyfriend, she can find one herself.

"Check your schudule. Maybe we're in the same level," Pilar tells Del.

"Actually, Pilar, he's in the top level with me," I say. I've never made a big deal of the fact that Pilar's in a lower level for math because it never mattered before. But I feel like showing her she isn't all that great.

"Oh, right," Pilar says. She looks a bit self-conscious, more like the old Pilar I knew, and hastily scoots down the corridor.

"Girls are so weird," Del says.

"What do you mean?"

"Well, you're obviously friends, but you don't seem to actually like each other," he says.

I shake my head. "You've got it the wrong way round. We're *not* friends anymore. But that's the problem because I do like Pilar—I like her a lot."

*　*　*

At lunchtime I leave Del in the playground with a soggy sandwich from the cafeteria and go to orchestra. I sit in my normal seat and practice scales to warm up my clarinet while I wait for Mr. Rowls and the rest of the band to come to practice. After a couple of minutes, Egan Winters, carrying his flute case, pushes open the music room doors.

"All right, Apple," he says. "It's Apple, isn't it?"

I nod.

"I love Macs. And iPhones. I always think it's funny when someone's got a cell that isn't an iPhone. You know?"

I nod again.

He pulls a chair next to me and sits down. "Your mum's nice. She seems really young."

"She's thirty-one," I tell him.

"Really? My parents are *old*, man. Mum is almost sixty, and Dad's sixty-five."

"I think my nan's sixty-five," I tell him, though I'm not sure why.

He looks at me and smiles. I can't tell whether it's one of those pitying smiles or a real one. "Right," he says. He takes out his flute and taps the keys.

"Mum is always having parties," I tell him. "She's having one on Saturday."

"Is it someone's birthday?"

"No. It's a Saturday night party with dancing and drinks," I say.

"Doesn't your dad mind?"

"My dad lives with my stepmum in London," I tell him.

Egan smiles. "I can't believe an eighth grader has a

better Saturday night than me." He blows some scales through his flute. They're clear and smooth, and his breath through the holes makes my hair stir.

I try to think about what Mum would do.

"You can come over for a drink. If you want." Even though I've spent the last few minutes carefully piecing my clarinet together and tuning it up, I pull the head joint off and polish it against my skirt.

Egan's eyes are on me. "Shouldn't you ask first?"

"It would be okay."

"Really? Could I bring a mate?" he asks.

My heart thunders. "'Course. If you want. The more the merrier. The flat's a bit of a mess at the moment though, 'cause we just moved in." I know I don't sound like myself. I'm not pronouncing all my letters. Nana would be horrified.

Egan doesn't notice. "All right then, you're on."

*　　*　　*

I float out of orchestra practice, and when I see Pilar and Donna by the basketball court talking to a group of ninth-grade boys and shrieking with laughter, I hardly care. They can all have each other. Egan Winters is coming to my house. He's going to be at a party *with me*.

178

It's like a dream, and it wouldn't be happening if Mum hadn't come back.

Del is on the bench where I left him. He's reading a book and ignoring the footballs barely missing him as they career out of the field and across the playground. They smack onto the wall behind him. "Hey," he says when I sit next to him. "How was glee club?"

"Great!" I say. I'm smiling so much my jaw aches.

"What lesson is next? I'm exhausted. I don't know how you run around these buildings all day."

I'd forgotten Del was homeschooled. "Is it scary being in a school?" I ask.

"Not scary. I just can't get used to having to carry my pens around with me."

I take out my planner. "We have English now. I think you'll like it," I say.

"Probably. I don't want to boast or anything, but I actually speak English fluently." Del nudges me with his elbow.

"I'm not so sure you do," I say. I laugh. It's a high-pitched, in-love kind of laugh, and if anyone saw us they might think I like Del. But I don't care what anyone thinks anymore. I'm so excited: Egan Winters is coming to my party.

*　*　*

At the beginning of English, Mr. Gaydon asks me for my homework. "I was absent yesterday, sir," I tell him. "That's why you don't have it."

"I know. Don't worry. Take a seat, Apple," he says.

I sit in the back corner with Del beside me.

Mr. Gaydon passes around a poem. "Right, here's what I have for you today. It's a piece by an American poet. Sadly she's been dead a while. Her name was Sara Teasdale. It's called 'Those Who Love.'" He beams and so do I. Most of the class grumble. "I know, I know, slushy love rubbish. But let me read you some of the words from the first stanza before you all start to gag." He sits up straight. "'Those who love the most; Do not talk of their love . . . or speak if at all; Of fragile inconsequent things.'" He pauses. "Isn't that interesting? I mean, right off the narrator is saying that if we love we don't necessarily go on and on about it."

"Thank God for that," Jim Joyce says.

"Could someone please read aloud the last stanza? Donna, will you do the honors?" Mr. Gaydon asks.

"I'm all right," Donna says. She folds her arms in front of her chest. I'd say she's still mad about Mr. Gaydon telling us war is pointless.

"I'll do it," Iona Churchill says.

"Thank you, Iona." Mr. Gaydon gets her to stand up and face everyone so we can all hear her. She begins:

"And a woman I used to know
Who loved one man from her youth,
Against the strength of the fates
Fighting in sombre pride
Never spoke of this thing,
But hearing his name by chance,
A light would pass over her face."

"What do you make of that bit of the poem then?" Mr. Gaydon asks.

His questions never have a fixed answer, so we do what we usually do in Mr. Gaydon's class—stare at him and try to think of something clever to say.

Mr. Gaydon points at Jim. "Mr. Joyce, do you love anyone?"

Jim tugs on the sleeves of his shirt. "Bit of a personal question, isn't it, sir? Don't know if you're allowed to ask us questions like that."

"He can ask us whatever he likes," Mackenzie Bainbridge bites back. "Can I answer, sir?"

Mr. Gaydon nods.

"My sister's name is Mandy, and she's at university. We text each other a hundred times a day, but I'm never like, 'Oh, Mandy, I love you, you're the best.' She just is."

Mr. Gaydon smiles. "Excellent, Mackenzie. Thank you."

I've never been in a class where telling the teacher that you love your sister could be an excellent answer, but Mr. Gaydon's like that—if you tell him something true, he's delighted.

"So what is the narrator saying about real love? Mackenzie gave us a big hint."

"It's boring," Jim Joyce says.

No one laughs. We like Mr. Gaydon now that we know him. We like him more than we like Jim.

Del throws his hand up.

Mr. Gaydon looks our way. "You're new," he says.

"New to the school, yes. Not new to the world. Very much established in my own life," Del says.

Pilar giggles. So do a few other girls. Jim Joyce does not look happy about this.

Mr. Gaydon gives Del a thumbs-up. "Fantastic to hear that. So what were you about to say?"

"Well, I think that the poem is about how love is quiet,

you know. The woman in that bit Iona read loves someone, but you wouldn't be able to guess unless you were watching her really closely. Basically, the poet means that you don't have to fly your sweetheart to Venice to show her you love her. Sometimes you can just buy someone a Toblerone chocolate bar."

"A Toblerone?" Mr. Gaydon asks.

"It's the triangle shapes that make it romantic."

Mr. Gaydon laughs. "What's your name?"

"Del Holloway."

"Well, I'm glad you're with us, Del."

For the rest of the lesson Mr. Gaydon gets us to imagine the woman from the poem and write her story. Del and I work together and set our story in the Scottish Highlands. The woman is a clan princess, and the man she loves is her best friend from childhood. Mr. Gaydon likes what we've written. He tells us it has a "strong emotional landscape," whatever that means.

But for homework he has a different assignment. "Write one hundred words about someone you love," he tells the class. "Someone you really love, not someone you think you love. Spend some time working out the difference."

I think about Egan Winters. I've been besotted with

him since I was in seventh grade. But I can't write about him. I'll have to think of someone else.

On the way out of class Mr. Gaydon calls me to his desk. "Apple, can I see you?"

Mr. Gaydon waits for everyone, including Del, to leave the room before speaking. "While the class was working on the stories today, I had a chance to look over your homework. It was very well written. I mean, it was beautiful. Do you ever write in your spare time?"

I shrug. Lately, I haven't had any spare time to do anything. And anyway, I know the piece I wrote about football fans wasn't very good. I didn't even spell-check it.

"Well, I'm impressed by your work. I want to read more. But I'm also concerned." He pauses. "Is everything okay?"

"Yes, sir."

"Really? Because I rather thought this was your way of asking for help." He hands me the paper with my homework on it. I scan the page. I can't believe it. The poem about Pilar and Donna is staring at me in black and white. The librarian printed out the wrong document.

I stuff it into my schoolbag. "That's not my

homework. That's something else. I wrote about foot-ball," I say.

Mr. Gaydon twiddles the hair at the end of one of his sideburns. "Would you like me to get all three of you girls together to sort this out?"

"No! I never meant you to read it."

He squints. "Hmm."

I can tell that he thinks I handed in the homework on purpose. But I don't need anyone's help. And I don't want Pilar and Donna thinking I'm so desperate I went to a teacher behind their backs.

"Can I go?" I ask.

I look at the door. Del is making faces through the round window.

"I want you to promise to come to me if it gets worse."

"I'm okay," I say.

"And I want you to take this." He reaches for a clean gray exercise book, identical to my English one. "It's for you to scribble down poems that come to you." I stare at the exercise book. "No need to look so glum. It isn't extra homework. It's for fun. And if you don't like it, no worries."

"Thank you," I say. I head for the door. "And sir?" I turn around.

"Yes?" He looks hopeful.

"Donna's dad is in Afghanistan. I think she's really proud of him. All that stuff about war we were doing probably made her upset with you."

Mr. Gaydon doesn't move. "Afghanistan?" he asks.

"Yes, sir," I say, and join Del in the corridor.

28

The rest of the week at school is worse than ever. Pilar looks horrified each time she bumps into me, and Donna does everything she can to make me feel left out—whispering behind her hand or laughing hysterically whenever I pass by. I make sure I don't flinch when she's mean. I won't let her think she's getting to me.

To stay cheerful I think about Saturday and how Egan Winters is coming to our place for drinks. When I tell Mum I've invited him, she gives me a high five.

"My girl! So we'll have to make this party extra cool."

"*Extra* cool," I say.

"I don't want another stupid party," Rain says. She's ironing Jenny's tiny clothes. She doesn't even iron her own clothes. None of us do.

"Oh, come on, it'll be good fun. I'll invite Pete. You like Pete," Mum says.

"Who's Pete?" The iron hisses and huffs.

"You know Pete. He's the one who does all the accents. He looks like the British prime minister."

"What's a prime minister?" Rain asks.

"The leader of a country," I tell her.

"Well, I'm American, how should I know that? We have presidents. Anyway, I don't want another party," she says.

"One last one, Rain. Then we're done with parties. Okay?" Mum says.

Rain pouts.

"We'll need drinks," I say.

"Alcohol? I don't want people saying I ply young boys with booze," Mum says.

"You ply Apple with booze," Rain snaps.

"Don't be cheeky, Rain." Mum scowls. It's a look she reserves for when Rain is being a real pain. She never looks at me like this, and even though it makes me feel special, and I like being a favorite, I can't help feeling sorry for Rain.

"Why don't we make cakes for the party, Rain?" I ask.

"You're only being nice because you're scared I'm going to spoil everything, and then you won't get to make out with that boy you've got a crush on."

"I don't want to make out with anyone."

Rain looks at me skeptically. "*Sure*."

Mum sits on the couch, tucks her bare feet under her bum, and turns on the TV. "We're having a party on Saturday whether you like it or not, so get over it."

Rain stomps off to our room.

"There she goes again," Mum says. "What's *wrong* with her?"

I unplug the iron and put it away. Watching Rain using it was making me nervous. "Maybe she should go back to the doctor," I say.

Mum nods. "Maybe. But I can't work out this country's health system at all. I think I have to register with a local doctor first or something."

"You do," I say. And she has to register me too, now that I don't live on the other side of town with Nana.

"What a drag. I need a beer. Get me one, would you, Apple," Mum says.

I go to the fridge and take out a cold green bottle. "Don't you want some spaghetti first?" I ask. I made it when I got home from school, so it's already gone cold.

Mum shakes her head. "No, thanks. I should've told

you that I'm not a fan of pasta. Do we have any chocolate cookies?"

I try to hide my disappointment. "We have custard creams," I say.

"Pass the packet here," Mum says. "And don't forget the beer."

29

By seven o'clock on Saturday we've laid out a spread of olives, cheeses, baguettes, and hummus. I'm so nervous I can't eat or drink anything. I'm wearing one of Mum's short black dresses with a pair of her high-heeled shoes again. Even though from the side you can see my stomach popping out, from the front I look okay.

Mum hands me a coral-colored lipstick. "Smack a bit of that on," she says. I go down to the bathroom to use the mirror.

Rain is in there. She's lying in the bath with Jenny. There is no water in the bath and they've both got clothes on, but it's obvious Rain's been crying; there are maroon circles beneath her eyes; her cheeks are dappled pink.

"What's happened?" I ask. I wish she could be normal for one night.

She turns Jenny's face to me. It's covered in red dots.

Rain asked to use my felt-tip pens earlier, and this must have been why. "Jenny's sick," she says.

"What?" I gaze at the limp doll in Rain's hands.

"We have to go to the hospital. She could have measles."

I want to scream and tell her that Jenny's only a plastic doll and that she's crazy for believing otherwise. Egan Winters will be here any minute, and she's basically ruining my life. But I don't scream or say any of those things because I know that would make it worse. The only way out of this is to be very nice to her.

"That's definitely not measles," I say. "It looks like an allergy."

"An allergy?" Rain examines the dots on Jenny's face like she's seeing them for the first time. Like she wasn't the one to put them there in the first place.

"Yeah. I had a rash a few days ago. I think it's because Mum bought that cheap washing powder."

"Laundry detergent?"

"Laundry detergent, exactly." I hold out my hands. "Give Jenny here to me a minute. I've got some spray in my schoolbag that'll make her all better. I promise."

"I'll get it," she says. She hands Jenny over, hops out of the bath, and pounds up the hall. Anyone would think she was seriously worried. It's so strange and sad I can't help holding the doll tight against me and kissing its head. She smells of Rain—a bit like cookies.

I lock the bathroom door and break off a few pieces of toilet paper. I poke around underneath the sink. When I find the nail polish remover, I soak the toilet paper with it and rub Jenny's face. Hard. I feel a bit bad—I'd hate to have someone rub nail polish remover all over my face. Then I think about Egan Winters who could be on his way up our stairs right this second and rub even harder. After a minute, Jenny's face is clean of marks and Rain is banging on the bathroom door.

"I'm peeing," I shout.

"I can't find any medicine in your bag," Rain says.

"It was actually in here all along. Wait a second." I squirt Mum's tulip-scented body spray over Jenny's face and rub it in with my thumbs. Then I flush the toilet and open the door.

"It's working already," I say. I hand Jenny over.

Rain sniffs. "What's that smell?"

"Huh?" I turn to the mirror and carefully dab my lips with the coral lipstick.

"Where's the medicine? Are you sure it's safe for babies?" Rain is studying Jenny's clear face, unbelieving.

"I'm sure. But I'm such a twit I managed to drop it in the toilet before I flushed it. I'll have to get some more."

When I turn around, Rain is examining me. She doesn't look afraid and miserable now. But she isn't happy either.

"What?" I ask.

She blinks. "Nothing," she says.

*　　*　　*

When Mum's friends arrive, they stand by the open window smoking cigarettes. The neighbors from downstairs, who Mum invited because they're students and would make the crowd seem a bit younger, sit on the kitchen counter drinking whisky and talking loudly about "the nature of reality." Egan Winters isn't here yet even though it's almost nine o'clock. Mum tells me not to worry. "He'll be here. I have a feeling," she says. "Where's your sister?"

"Jenny wasn't well, so . . ."

"Be careful or she'll have you convinced that thing's real," Mum says.

At that moment Egan Winters appears at the top of our stairs along with two other senior boys

Mum charges toward them and throws her arms

around Egan. He smiles awkwardly. I totter over in my heels.

"This is Andrew and that's Dean," Egan says.

His friends grunt.

"Come on in. It's a horrible night out there, isn't it? Glad you could make it. Now, what's it to be, beer or wine?" Mum asks.

"Beer," Egan says.

"Yeah, beer," the other two say.

Mum turns and bumps into me as she goes to get the drinks. "Egan's here," she says.

Egan looks at me, taking in what I'm wearing. His eyes linger on my chunky legs for a second. I pull at the hem of the dress.

"All right?" he says.

I nod. "Yeah." And we stand in silence until Mum comes back with three wet beer bottles.

"How did you get here?" Mum asks.

"I just passed my test, so I drove," Egan says. He looks at his beer guiltily. "I'll have half this bottle."

"Do I look like the police?" Mum says. She's trying to be funny, and even though there isn't anything funny about drunk driving, Andrew and Dean laugh and nudge each other.

Egan is looking at Mum with a half smile. I can't tell

if that means he thinks she's cool or something else. That's the only bad thing about Egan Winters—you can never tell what he's thinking.

I stand listening while Mum keeps the boys entertained. They talk about cars and music and films, and it's all great because they're in *my* flat and talking to *my* mum, but I don't get half of what they're saying: the films are all R-rated, which I haven't seen; I never listen to music except boy band stuff that Pilar has on her iPhone; and I don't drive. I probably seem like a stupid kid in my mum's clothes, trying to act like a grown-up.

"I'm going to mix myself a cocktail. Anyone want one?" I ask.

The boys all look at their beers and shake their heads. "If you're making calimocho, sign me up," Mum says. "Go easy on the Coke."

I make two glasses of calimocho, one with extra red wine for Mum. When I get back to the huddle, Egan Winters is telling her about where he wants to go to university. Warwick, apparently, which I've never heard of. "My brother goes there, so I've visited it loads," he explains.

"That's *swell*," Mum says, her American accent coming out again. She's probably bored listening to Egan

Winters, but you can't tell. She looks completely captivated, which makes him talk and talk and talk. I'm not used to hearing his voice, but it's nice—deep and kind of soft for a boy, like what he's saying is really serious even when he's talking about something that isn't. His two friends aren't chatty. Andrew finishes his beer quickly, then stands chewing on a crust of baguette. Dean grabs another beer and is already halfway through it.

Someone waving a cigarette calls Mum to the window. "I gotta mingle. You guys help yourselves to drinks and food. You'll be safe with Apple," Mum says. She gives me this long look. I know I'm meant to understand what it means, but I don't. When she wanders off, I stand there speechless.

"Do you want some olives?" I ask.

Egan chews his bottom lip, almost twitchily, and finishes his beer. I've never been close enough to notice his eyes before—creamy brown like freshly fallen chestnuts. "We stopped for kebabs before we got here," Egan says. "Can I have a Coke or something?"

"Yes, yes, of course," I say. I almost fall over, clambering to the fridge to get him a can before he changes his mind and goes home.

He takes it from me and flicks the ring pull. "Got a glass?"

"Oh yeah, sorry."

"I'll get it, don't worry," he says. He puts his hand on my arm, and my stomach clenches. He goes off to find a glass. But he doesn't come back and stand with me; he edges his way to the window where Mum and her smoking friends are laughing and clinking glasses. After a few minutes he is laughing and clinking with them. I'm stuck with his friends who are now on to the subject of video games. They are comparing tactics for getting through early levels of a game I've never heard of. It's as dull as it can get, and even though I'm trying to be polite, I just want to be with Egan and Mum. When there's a pause in the conversation, I tell them I have to go and check on my sister, and sneak off to the bathroom to reapply my lipstick.

It's dark, and I almost scream when I close the bathroom door and turn on the light. Rain is perched on the toilet. Luckily the seat is down, but she's unwound all the toilet roll and is sitting with half of it on her lap. Her eyes are bloodshot. She's been crying again. "You've got to stop hiding in here. It's creeping me out," I hiss.

"I told you before that if you don't like how it is, you should go back to your nana." She blows her nose on her sleeve. Jenny's not with her.

Anger blisters through me. I've been nice to her all day,

and she repays me by being nasty. "I'm not going any-where," I say. "So you'd better get used to it."

"Mom only prefers you because you're new. When she's bored, she'll dump you and I'll be the favorite again. When we were in America, she never mentioned you. She told everyone I was her only child."

I feel like I've been punched in the guts. Maybe this is true, but I didn't want to know it.

My eyes sting. I bite my thumb to stop myself from crying. Looking in the mirror, I paste on the lipstick as thick as I can. Mum's left her makeup on the sink. I brush a bit of mascara through my eyelashes and dab some creamy blush on my cheeks too.

"Is that boy here?" Rain asks.

I ignore her and inspect my legs. They're pale and lumpy above the knee.

"When is everyone going home?" Rain asks. Her voice has lost its sharp edge.

"Put that toilet roll back on the holder. It's all we've got left," I tell her and storm off.

In the sitting room, Mum, Egan, and her smoking friends are now sitting in a circle on the floor. Loads of other guests have joined them, including Andrew and Dean.

When Mum sees me, she waves me over. "We're

playing Truth or Dare. I'm terrified this bottle's going to make us all give away our PIN numbers!"

I sit next to Mum on the carpet. My dress rides up. I watch Merlin spin the empty wine bottle.

"Truth or dare?" I ask. It looks scarily like a game of Spin the Bottle.

"You spin it, and whoever it lands on has to answer your question or do a dare," Mum says.

The bottle stops spinning and points at Gina. She rolls her eyes.

Merlin rubs his hands together. "Truth or dare?" he asks.

"This is stupid. I'm not telling you lot anything!" Gina says.

"If you didn't want to play, you shouldn't have sat down!" Mum says. She doesn't seem to be able to keep her calimocho in the glass, and it sloshes all over my legs. "Sorry, love," she says, wiping away the spill with a corner of her silk scarf.

Mum gulps down the rest of the glass and points it at Gina. "When was the last time you picked your nose?" she says. She hoots like this is the funniest thing ever. Andrew and Dean hoot too. It's a bit like being in primary school.

"Not fair. It's my question," Merlin says. No one is listening to him.

"Today!" Gina says, and sticks her middle finger right up her nose. Everyone falls over laughing. I can't help giggling a bit.

"My turn," Mum says. She leans for the bottle and spins it so hard it slides across the floor. We all watch it slow down until it stops. And it's pointing at Egan. I stiffen. Mum extends her arm as far forward as she can. She makes little circles with her finger in Egan's face.

Egan locks eyes with Mum.

"Truth or dare?" Mum asks.

Egan pushes his hair out of his face. His chestnut eyes glint in the light. "Go on then, dare me to do something," he says. He smiles and rubs the end of his nose. He doesn't look frightened.

Mum glances around the room, looking for an idea. Then she points at me. "I dare you to kiss Apple," she says.

Everyone screeches. They think this is the funniest thing they've ever heard. Gina rolls on the floor in hysterics.

But Egan isn't laughing. He is gazing at me.

"You chose a dare," Mum says. She leans in to me and whispers, "Is this the best party or what?"

I wait for Egan to say no. *No way.* I wait for him to tell Mum she's unhinged and inappropriate and stand up and storm out of the party. I don't know how I'll ever show my face at orchestra again. It's too much.

I drop my head in my hands.

Then I hear Egan's voice. "No biggie," he says.

I look up.

"Are you serious, mate? She's eleven," Dean says.

"She's fourteen," Mum says.

"Fourteen's all right," Andrew says. He elbows Egan, egging him on.

Egan gets on his hands and knees and crawls forward. Before I know what's happening, his face is so close I can see every little fleck in his eyes like pieces of stars. His breath still smells of the beer.

And then it happens.

Egan's lips touch mine.

They're warm and wet, and after a second he presses them harder. My stomach flips, but not in a happy or excited way. I think I'm going to be sick. I inhale deeply as he pulls away. He wipes his mouth on his sleeve.

"There," he says. He gulps down some Coke.

Everyone cheers.

Mum claps. "Well done, Egan. You can come to all our parties."

I am unable to move. I don't know what's happened. I've kissed Egan Winters, or *he's* kissed *me*. And even though it's what I've dreamed about for such a long time, it wasn't private or special or anything I imagined it would be. It was a joke, and everyone was watching. It was a game.

And it was horrible.

I want to run away. I want to shout at Mum for making this happen.

Andrew and Dean are squawking like a pair of parakeets. Andrew smacks Egan on the back like he's just won an Olympic medal. Egan Winters is looking at me carefully, almost apologetically.

I sit really still and focus hard on the swirls in the old red carpet. If I get up straightaway, everyone will know I'm upset. I don't want them to think I'm a spoilsport. I wait until the bottle has been spun a few times, then sneak off to my bedroom.

Rain is snoring and has one leg hanging over the side of her bunk. I turn off the light and crawl in under my duvet, still wearing my dress and shoes. I don't know how Rain can sleep: the music sounds like it's coming from speakers in our room. No matter how far I push my fingers into my ears, I can still hear it booming. I wish everyone would go home.

I curl into a tight ball, and eventually I must manage to fall asleep, because when I open my eyes the flat is quiet.

I creep into the sitting room. Mum's sleeping on the couch fully clothed. A cigarette is smoldering in an empty wine glass. I stub it out and pull off Mum's boots. One of her big toes is poking through a hole in her tights.

All the lights have been left on, and the window is still wide open. Icy air whistles through the flat.

I close and lock the window and fill the dishwasher with as many glasses and dishes as I can fit into it—if I don't turn it on, we'll have nothing clean to eat or drink from tomorrow.

On the floor is a blue baseball cap. Egan's. I lift it to my nose and sniff. It smells of sweat, like any other hat would. I put it on my head and wipe down the counter-top, dusty with ash.

Mum stirs. "Apple? Why did you disappear? Everyone was asking for you."

"I got tired, Mum."

"I don't blame you." She yawns and sits up. "Egan

wanted to thank you for the party. I told him it was all your idea."

"Really?"

Mum stands up. "Yeah. I think he likes you."

"No, he doesn't."

"He kissed you."

"But it was a dare."

"If I dared you to kiss Merlin, would you?" she asks.

I imagine Merlin's long, shiny nose touching mine. "No way."

Mum stands up and yawns again. She covers her mouth with the back of her hand. "I'm exhausted. And I've got to call a load of agents tomorrow." She makes for the corridor. "I'll go to bed." She blows me a kiss and disappears.

I'm left to switch out the lights and turn on the dishwasher. It's not a big deal. It's just some switches and buttons. But it feels like a big deal.

For some reason, it feels like a really big deal.

30

I promise Rain that if she comes with me to church, I'll make her a hot chocolate with cream later that day. She smiles for the first time all weekend and puts Jenny into the baby carrier. I forgot to set an alarm, so even though we jog all the way, we're late. *Really* late. The priest is already giving his sermon.

Nana turns and sees us slide into a back pew. Her hair is sprayed into a high puff that doesn't move when she does. I expect her to be angry because I'm so late, but she smiles gently and turns back to face the altar.

After Mass, we wait at the back of the church for Nana. Father Doherty sees me and pats my head. "What have I done to upset you now, wee one? I've had no one to bring up the offertory since you've been away." Father Doherty is Irish like Nana. But he's from a different part—a place called Belfast—and he sounds like he still lives there. Sometimes he speaks so quickly, I can't understand what he's saying.

"I moved in with my mum, father."

"Aye, sure I know, your granny told me about that. And how's it going anyway?"

"Good," I say.

"That was a lovely sermon, father." It's Nana. Father Doherty pulls Nana toward him and kisses her on the cheek. Father Doherty's not like some of the other priests who stand on the altar like they're God themselves. His sermons are always about how he did the wrong thing but then learned from it. Whenever I listen to him, I wonder what I could learn from my mistakes, but I'm not as clever as Father Doherty—I can't turn my life into lessons.

"Oh no, don't tell me, there's Mrs. Baker. She's been after me to help her organize a jumble sale. I'm going to scoot off and hide," Father Doherty says, and away he goes.

Nana pecks my cheek with dry lips. "Hello," she says. She's almost shy.

"Hi, Nana." We hardly look at each other. It's stupid because we've lived our whole lives in the same house. There's no reason for us to feel uneasy.

Nana bends down, so she's eye to eye with Rain. "I'm glad you came too."

Rain knits her eyebrows together. She holds on to my coat.

"Come on. I've a lovely piece of pork and lots of potatoes roasting in the oven," Nana says.

* * *

Nana's roasts are the best. The potatoes are always crunchy on the outside and soft in the middle. Her meat is never chewy. She makes her own applesauce, which she calls "Apple's applesauce," and she makes the gravy from meat juices, not a can.

Rain eats like she's never had a meal before. She stuffs half a potato into her mouth. Before she's finished it, she stuffs some carrots in too. She forgets Jenny who is lying alone on the couch, Derry sniffing around her.

Nana watches Rain but doesn't criticize her manners like she would if I ate like that.

"How are things going?" Nana asks during dessert—homemade coffee and walnut cake with double cream.

"Fine," I say. Derry comes in and rubs my leg with his nose. I break off a piece of cake, hide it, and hold it out for him beneath the table. He lathers my hand in spit.

"Fine? That it?" Nana asks.

"It's great," I say.

"Your mum's well? She likes having two daughters to contend with?"

"Mum's a natural," I tell her.

"Your dog's licking my knees," Rain says. She giggles.

Nana shoos Derry away. "He's getting cheeky, that one. Been a bit spoiled since you left. So tell me, how do you like Brampton-on-Sea, Rain? Is school fun?"

Rain answers without looking up. "I don't go to school." I was so worried about Rain telling Nana about the parties and Egan Winters, I forgot to tell her to keep the school thing a secret.

Nana puts down her spoon. "Really?" she asks breezily.

"The teachers and kids were mean about Jenny."

"Right," Nana says. When Rain used the bathroom earlier, I had a chance to tell Nana that Rain thinks Jenny's real. She asked whether Mum's taken her to see a doctor about it. I said she had, which is true; I just didn't tell her when or where Rain saw this doctor. "So what do you do all day?"

"I stay with Mom. Sometimes Apple takes care of me." She shovels the last piece of muddy-colored cake into her mouth.

A cloud appears across Nana's face.

"That's not true. I stayed off one day," I say.

"Well, I don't think you should be staying off any day. You've always had one hundred percent attendance at school, Apple." It's true. Last year I got a certificate for it. I won't get one this year though.

"It was *one day*," I say.

"Well, so long as one day doesn't become two days and then three days." Her voice is stony and strict, how I remember it, but when she turns to Rain, she's sweet again. "And what about you, pet? How do you learn, if you aren't at school?"

Rain pours more cream onto her plate. "Apple took me to the library. I got out some books."

Nana sighs. "I see."

"What do you see?" I ask, because I know she doesn't see. It's typical of Nana not to understand—to make a big deal of nothing and make it seem like Mum's the devil.

"I think Annie and I have to talk," Nana says.

I stand up. "We should go now, Rain. Come on."

"Sit down and wait for your mother to pick you up," Nana tells me.

"She doesn't have a car," Rain says.

"Rain!" I shout. I can't help it. She's giving Nana ammunition to use against Mum, which will lead to more arguments. All I want is for Nana and Mum to be friends, so I can see them both without feeling sticky with guilt.

I rush to the hall and wait for Rain. Nana follows. She takes my hand and makes me look at her. "Apple, what's going on?"

My eyes brim with tears. I don't know why. "Everything's fine."

Nana rubs her eyebrows with the tips of her fingers. "Then why are you running away from me?"

"We'll come again soon," Rain says. She's got Jenny back in the carrier.

"Yes, we'll come soon, Nana," I say, and dash after my sister, who is skipping down the steps, full of cake and potatoes.

31

Not having anyone to eat lunch with is the worst thing about Pilar dumping me, and it's not like I can even hang around with Del because he's signed himself up as a library monitor. So I stop going into the cafeteria. On the way to school I buy chips and a doughnut and eat them on a bench behind the music room. The only day I don't dread is Tuesday, when orchestra practice takes up most of the lunch period and I don't have to be alone.

I get to the music room before anyone else and head into the cupboard for a chair and music stand, when people scrape into the room. The stands are hidden behind a pile of tambourines. I'm about to drag one out when I hear Egan Winters's voice.

"I think I'll go over and see her after school," he says.

"You're mad, mate!" It's Andrew. He doesn't play an

instrument. Sometimes he just comes to orchestra with Egan to eat lunch. I suspect he also likes ogling the eleventh-grade girls playing cello.

Egan lowers his voice. "Look, the age difference matters less the older you get. In a few years it wouldn't seem that much."

My heart thrashes against my ribs like a frightened bird in a cage. The age difference? Could he be talking about me? Could he be talking about *us*? My breathing becomes so loud I wonder whether he can hear me. The rest of the horrible school day washes away, and I feel like a rainbow is creeping into my shoes and spinning its way up my legs, into my belly, my chest, my head.

"Even if she fancied you, I think it's illegal. Why don't you find someone in our year. What about Sara Watts?" Andrew says.

Egan makes a sound like he's being sick. "Sara? Uh, no thanks. You ask her out, if you like her so much. And good luck getting her to brush those teeth." I'm so happy I almost let out a giggle. I press my forearm against my mouth to stifle it. Egan continues. "My only problem is Apple."

My hands fall to my sides. His problem? How? I like him too. Doesn't he know that?

"You shouldn't have kissed her, mate. Seriously. Firstly, it was well dodgy. And secondly, it was obvious she thought it was for real. I bet it was her first kiss. You have that on your conscience," Andrew says.

"It was a dare," Egan says. "And in case you've forgotten, you egged me on."

I know I've misunderstood something. He isn't talking about me at all. He's talking about someone else.

"If she liked you, she wouldn't let you kiss her daughter," Andrew says.

The rainbow in my belly fizzles out. A heavy rock replaces it.

"She wanted to see if I was a laugh. Anyway, she was so high, she'd have done anything. I wish she had." Egan laughs. Andrew does too.

I crumple onto the floor. The tambourines behind me clink and clash.

"What's that?" Egan says.

He appears at the cupboard door.

I stand up unsteadily, race out of the cupboard, and grab my schoolbag.

"Apple, wait!" Egan says.

"Oh, mate, you're in trouble now," Andrew says. He bites into a Mars bar.

Egan puts his flute on the floor and comes to me.

I root in my schoolbag. I find his cap and throw it at him. "This has been stinking up our flat," I say.

"Look, I'm sorry. I didn't know you were in here."

"You fancy my *mum*? She's in her thirties, and she told me that she thinks you're immature and stupid," I say. "Anyway, she's got a boyfriend. He's rich and he drives a Porsche and he's . . . an architect. So you haven't got a chance."

Egan goes pale. "Oh. Yeah. I mean, I didn't really think . . . you know. Andrew and I were messing around."

I don't wait to hear any more. I have to go home.

I storm out of the music room, across the playground, and into the nurse's office. I tell her I have the worst period pains ever. She asks all the usual questions, like what classes I have and whether I've had an argument with someone. When she's satisfied with my lies, she calls Mum to pick me up. But Mum can't because she hasn't got a car. So I walk.

*   *   *

At home Mum is lying on the couch watching TV. "Hey, sweets. I've got painkillers in my bag, if you need them."

"I'm okay," I say. I sit next to her.

"You're sweating. Have you got a temperature?" She places the back of her hand against my forehead.

"Mum, would you go out with someone who was seventeen?"

She laughs.

"I'm being serious."

"I went out with a seventeen-year-old once, Apple. That was your dad. I think he was enough for me."

"Right," I say.

"Is everything okay?" she asks. She yanks off my coat.

I don't want to tell her about Egan Winters. It's too humiliating. I don't want her to think I'm a loser. And if I'm honest, a small part of me worries that maybe she likes Egan Winters too—if I tell her how he feels maybe she'll run off with him. Or worse, bring him home and make him my stepdad.

"How's Rain?" I ask to divert the conversation.

Mum tuts. "Apparently Jenny's got a cough. She's been nagging me to take her to see a nurse."

"It would be a good excuse to get Rain to the doctor," I say.

"Maybe," Mum says. She turns up the volume on the TV. "I reckon I'd win a lot, if I could get a spot on a game show. They're all dipsticks." She pushes my hair away from my face and kisses my cheek.

"Shall I put the kettle on?" I ask.

"You know what, a white wine would be lovely," she says. She turns to the TV. "Open box seventeen. *Seventeen*!"

32

I told Nana that I only missed a day of school. I made it seem like a one-off. But on Wednesday I skip school again. Mum has a casting call in London for a part in *The Woman in Black* and she can't wait for Rain, who spends ages getting showered and then, just before Mum's about to leave, says Jenny's done a "mammoth poop" and needs changing.

Mum waves her arms around and shouts so loudly, I worry she might hit Rain. "You know perfectly well that if I leave you here alone and someone finds out, I'll have child welfare on my back. Do you want to go into a foster home? Is that what you want?" She's screaming at Rain, but she's looking at me.

"I'll take care of her," I say. I'd do almost anything to avoid going back to school.

When Mum's gone, I clear up the breakfast dishes, put

some towels and bedsheets in for washing, and do my homework. I start with English. Mr. Gaydon asked us to write about someone we love. It only takes me a minute to decide what to write about.

"Someone I Thought I Loved" by Apple Apostolopoulou

I thought a kiss meant
Everything.
I thought it meant love—
Until He kissed me.
His mouth was moist, his breath like beer,
His face so close I saw the fear
Of me and what I was.
Not the girl I wanted to be
But just
A Girl.
A Child.
A Silliness
To him,
And to everyone else who laughed
At the performance.
My nana always said that
Love is an action.

I know now she didn't mean kissing
Or anything close to it.
She meant that love is quiet doing—
A day to day toil in the dark.

Rain peers over my shoulder. "What are you writing?" she asks. She reads the first line and laughs. "Have you written about that boy Egan? Have you written about how you *love* him?"

I slam down the lid of my laptop. "Get out of my life, can't you?"

Rain snorts. "Love poetry is so *lame*," she says.

"Don't you have something to do?"

She shakes her head.

"We've got to take the library books back, so go and read them," I tell her.

Rain curls up on the couch with a book about Elizabeth the First. I open the laptop and a fresh document, so I can do my homework for real.

"Someone I Love" by Apple Apostolopoulou

Mallary Ford is the best writer on the planet. She writes like she can see inside people, especially people

my age. My nana encourages me to play the clarinet,
but when I leave school, I would like to write
children's books. My dream is to be as good as
Mallary Ford (although I doubt that will ever
happen). I have never met Mallary Ford, but if I did I
would probably have to curtsy in front of her. Maybe
people think you can't love someone you do not
know, but you can love someone's work; I think that's
close enough.

Rain stands behind me again.

"Stop bloody spying on me!" I shout.

"I finished the books," she says.

"*All* the books?" I sound like a teacher.

"I skipped a few pages of the science one. I'm not interested in minerals."

"Fair enough."

*   *   *

In the library we swap the books we've read for fresh ones, renew the ones we still want, and borrow a couple of DVDs, which help to whittle away the afternoon. And happily, Mum gets home early. On the way she's picked up a pizza, half with olives for me, half with mushrooms and pepperoni for Rain. I know Nana wouldn't approve of me missing school, but it's worth it because Mum's found a part in a play.

"It's only a few lines, but it's in the West End and it's a foot in the door. I start in three weeks. Finally we'll have *some* money coming in." She kicks off her shoes and rubs her feet.

"That's fantastic. Congratulations!" I hug her quickly. I can hardly believe my mum's a real actress.

"I knew you'd be pleased. Now, we're left with one problem." Mum glances at Rain. "If I'm to get more parts . . ."

"She has to go back to school," I say, finishing her sentence for her.

Rain has demolished her pizza. She is kneeling at the coffee table, cutting pictures from the John Lewis catalog and putting together a design for a nursery. "Are you talking about me?" she says.

"Of course not. We're talking about one of Apple's teachers," Mum says. She lowers her voice. "The school simply can't cope with her problem. I can hardly cope myself. You seem to be the only one she responds to."

"Me?"

"I bet that after a few more weeks of you living with

us, she'll get rid of that doll and settle down. She's got a sister now. Why would she need Jenny?"

I'm not sure Mum's right. Rain's been devoted to her doll today—taking her everywhere, even to the toilet. She's been announcing every cough or hiccup Jenny makes.

"I know this might seem a big thing to ask, Apple, but would you consider looking after her while I go to a few more auditions in London? I really think I could get some TV work if I persevere. You could help me out for a few days until I line up a babysitter? I don't really have a lot of disposable cash right now."

Mum doesn't have to convince me. I'll do anything to help her become a famous actress. In any case, I'd rather stay at home and watch films than spend all day avoiding Donna, Pilar, and Egan.

"I can take care of her," I say.

Mum hugs me so tight she almost breaks my neck. "Really? Oh, Apple, you're the best daughter *ever*."

Rain looks up then quickly gets back to cutting out pictures. But the brief, sad glance is unmistakable: it's the look of a daughter desperate for her mum to love her the best.

PART 5
disappointment

33

It takes Mum longer to find a babysitter for Rain than she expected. A few days off school turns into a week. A week turns into two. I worry that the school might send over a social worker to make sure Mum hasn't tied me to a radiator, but no one shows up. Rain and I are free to do as we please. Occasionally we make cupcakes or cookies and some of them turn out really nice, which makes me think of Nana. Mostly we just read and watch films.

One afternoon I read the Emily Dickinson book from the library, pages and pages of poems without stopping, and without really knowing what all of them mean. But it doesn't matter. I like the big dashes the poet uses and the random capital letters; it makes me think that if someone famous can beat up punctuation and get away with it, there's hope for me.

Then I read a line that makes me stop.

Tell all the Truth but tell it slant—

I think about the homework I've been doing for English and what rubbish it's all been. I scan the rest of the poem and at the end are more lines like that:

The Truth must dazzle gradually
Or every man be blind—

I think Dickinson is saying that you should tell the truth but that there's no need to be direct—you can show it from different angles so it won't be so shocking or hard to bear. Mr. Gaydon would know the correct meaning of the poem, and I start wishing I were in school so I could ask him. But if I did ask him, he would only make me work it out myself anyway, and he'd find something positive to say about whatever answer I came up with.

Then I remember the exercise book he gave me especially for my poems and pull it from my schoolbag. I run my hand over the smooth gray cover. A new exercise book always feels so full of promise, even when it's for a subject you don't like. I use a sharp pencil to write my name on the cover and open it at the first, clean page. I have no idea what to write, but that doesn't seem to matter. Words, dashes, and capital letters come out of nowhere:

Under the promise of Love
We give away ourselves—
And in the morning wonder
What's left lying on the shelves
Of rescued Spirit's end—
Under the shape of Love
We idle for the Future—
So bright and so surprising
Where nothing can be bitter
Or turned into a Better.

I like the rhythm of the words and shape of the poem and though I'm not sure exactly what it is I'm saying, I keep writing.

I write and write and write and only stop when Rain looks up from her own book and says, "Time for beans on toast."

"Definitely," I say. I shut the exercise book and head to the kitchen.

On my second Friday in a row off school, after Rain and I have raided the library and watched two animated films and three episodes of *Doctor Who*, we stroll down to the seafront. Seagulls nip at old plastic bottles left behind on the beach. A man with a metal detector scours the sand for treasure. It's drizzling as usual.

"Jenny's getting wet. Do you think she could get pneumonia?" Rain asks.

"No," I say.

The man with the metal detector fingers the sand, then pops something into his pocket.

"What about bronchitis?" Rain asks.

"Jenny's fine," I say. Every few hours Rain thinks of a new ailment for Jenny. Sometimes she gets so worked up, it's a struggle to stop her from calling an ambulance.

"Did you know that in Victorian times, one in three children died before they reached five years old?" Rain asks.

"I didn't know that," I say.

"It's true. I read about it in one of the library books. What do you think it is nowadays? One in ten?"

I sigh. Sometimes being Rain's babysitter is tiring. "I think I can say with one hundred percent certainty that Jenny is not at risk of catching anything life-threatening." I don't add that being plastic makes it impossible.

"But . . ."

"Why don't we get some fries?" I say.

In the fries shop I smother my portion with salt and vinegar.

Rain sticks out her tongue. "That's totally gross."

"It's delicious," I tell her.

"I want mine plain."

"Suit yourself."

We take our open fries to the promenade and sit on a damp bench. Rain doesn't make conversation, and neither do I. We watch the waves lap the sand, the gulls squawk, and a pair of cocker spaniels bark at the man's metal detector. I throw a handful of fries into the sky. A few seagulls swoop in to catch them. Rain pretend-screams.

"Can I sit with you?" It's Del Holloway. He's standing behind us with his own bag of open fries.

"It's you," I say. He's wearing a black shirt and tie and a gray felt hat. "Are you being homeschooled again?"

He puts a very large fry into his mouth. "Nope. Mum's great-aunt Lulu died, so we were at the funeral. Mum let me have the whole day off on account of my grief." He puts his hand over his heart and whines. "Can I sit down?"

"If you want," I say. I shift sideways, closer to Rain. "So, you weren't close to your aunt Lulu?"

"My *mum's great*-aunt Lulu. No, never met her," he says.

"I'm sorry anyway," I say.

"So, I haven't seen you at school. Did you transfer somewhere else?"

"Kind of," I say.

"Where are you now?"

I don't know why it's any of his business, but I tell him anyway. I can't help telling Del things. "My mum needed help with something."

"I miss you," he says quickly. He stuffs in a few more fries.

"What are you talking about?"

"Nothing. Just saying," Del leans across me and shakes Rain's hand. "I'm Del," he says.

"I'm Rain," she says.

"Rain is my long-lost sister—she's from America,

hence the weird accent," I tell him. "And Rain, this is Del, my old neighbor and general nosey parker."

Rain pretends to feed her doll a fry. "Is Jenny allowed fries?" I ask, forgetting for a second that Jenny isn't real.

"She's fine," Rain says. She props Jenny up on one knee and jiggles her. "This is Jenny. She's almost seven months old. A bit of a handful."

He nods like it's completely normal to act as though a doll's a real person. He even makes a face at Jenny, who stares back at him under her nylon eyelashes.

The rain comes down harder. None of us moves from the bench. We watch the gulls and cocker spaniels.

"Is Pilar one of the reasons you won't come back to school?" Del asks.

"I don't know what you mean," I say.

"Well, she told me you used to be friends."

"So, you and Pilar are having heart-to-hearts? Is she your girlfriend?"

He raises one eyebrow. "I don't think so. Do you?" He leans across me again and taps Rain's knee. "You and the baby wanna play the slots?"

Rain swats him away. "What are slots?"

"Seriously, don't say you've never played a slot machine. America's so backward."

"Have *you*?" I ask him. He wouldn't pass for fourteen, let alone eighteen.

"'Course I have. I'm a master gambler. Last year I won thirty thousand pounds on the gaming tables. Took ten grand off a professional boxer at poker. He threatened to beat me up, but then he saw my muscles." Del raises his fists. "You think I'm full of it, but I'm completely serious. Now come on."

I don't want to follow Del. I always get the feeling when I'm with him that he sees me too clearly. Not that he knows stuff *about* me, more that he just knows me— that he sees me more than I want him to. But before I can object, Rain's gamboling behind him toward the promenade arcades. I've no option but to get up and slog after them.

All arcades are the same: claw cranes suspended over stuffed, lime-green frogs and dance machines booming out beats. Everything invites us to *WIN WIN WIN*. The binging and jangling is deafening.

But Rain is mesmerized. And she doesn't seem to be worrying too much about how the noise might affect Jenny. I could mention it and we could go home, but if she's got her toe in the real world, I won't spoil it.

"Look!" Rain says. She stops by a machine with coins teetering along two ledges. It looks like it will throw the money out if it gets only a tiny nudge. "Let's play this one," she says.

Del presses his nose against the machine. The top ledge slides forward and backward. "It's not even close to coughing up," he says.

"The money's ready to drop," Rain says.

"Believe me," he says.

Rain doesn't argue. We continue along the promenade until we reach a rundown arcade called Captain Flame's Games. It's got an eight-foot peeling pirate standing guard outside. The parrot on his shoulder spins and screeches *Who's a clever boy then!* over and over and over.

At the back of the arcade is a row of ancient-looking slot machines. Del stops. Four men prod and smash the buttons. The machines whistle and moan. Five slot machines are free. Del doesn't make a move for any of them. "Let's pretend to play something else for now," he says. He points at a grabber filled with cheap pink teddies of different sizes and puts twenty pence into the slot. "Don't let me down!" he tells Rain, standing aside and offering her the lever.

The mechanical hand shudders. Rain smiles. "Can someone hold Jenny?"

Del grabs the doll and kisses it. "Come here to Uncle

Del, petal. Now, no crying, for goodness' sake. Momma's right there."

I give him a what-the-hell-are-you-on-about look. He pats the doll and squashes his face against the glass to gaze in at the teddies.

Rain holds the lever. She watches the hand glide along the metal rail. Once she has it in position, she yanks the lever toward her and the mechanical hand plunges into the pink pool of fuzz. I don't expect her to win anything, no one ever does, but a huge teddy dangles from the hand and within a couple of seconds is sliding out of the machine.

"I won!" Rain says.

Del looks as surprised as I do. "Crikey O'Reilly!" he says.

He grabs the teddy and lifts it in the air like a trophy. "Winners!" he shouts. "Question is, who does it belong to? See, technically you won it. But it was my money. Apple, what do you think? Mediate like this is a divorce settlement or something."

Rain's eyes are wide and anxious. She can't tell that Del is joking.

"Don't torture her," I say.

"But pink's my favorite color." He winks at Rain. "All

right, you have it. But don't let him bully Jenny. He looks like a brute."

"Thanks," Rain says. She squeezes the teddy for a second. Then she sees Jenny in Del's arm and reaches for her too. "Jenny can have him," she says.

Del glances over at the slot machines. One of the men is walking away. "No payout," Del says. "Perfect. Let's play."

"You were waiting for one of them to give up?" I ask.

"Yup. Oldest trick in the book. The machines all pay out eventually. Rigged, aren't they? Let's see how much that bloke's left behind."

We step up to the machine. Del pushes back his sleeves. I can't be sure under the dark lighting, but I think his watch is pink.

He sees me looking and taps it. "Told you it was my favorite color. I don't lie."

Rain is already by Del's side. Her eyes are glued to the buttons and lights. "What does it do anyway? The other ones are better. You can win toys. Why don't we play on them?"

Del grips the slot machine with two hands. He strokes it with his thumbs. "What you have to understand is that all the other games are a bit of fun, but a slot"—he takes a deep breath—"it requires respect. It's not about having fun. It's about making some wonga. Want to make some wonga?"

"You mean money?" Rain asks.

He lowers his voice so I almost can't hear him over the din. "Cash." He reaches into a trouser pocket, but when he pulls out his hand, he's only got a bunch of coppers. "Ah, Houston, we have a hitch."

"You've no money," I say.

"Can you loan me a pound?"

"I haven't got any money," I say.

"You've got the change from the fries," Rain says.

"But Mum'll want it back."

Del puts his arm around my shoulder like we're old friends. He smells of vinegar. "And you'll get it back. That and five more. I promise."

I rummage in my pocket and pull out the change, still wrapped in its receipt. I've two pound coins and two pennies. "I don't want more back, but if you lose it, you owe me."

"Deal!"

Del pops the pound coins into the slot. The slot machine comes to life with a riot of pings. The wheels in the machine spin. The buttons below them flash as if we've already won something. Del limbers up by putting his hands on his shoulders and making circles with his elbows. "Ready?" he asks.

"Go!" Rain says.

Del smacks one button. He waits until a wheel stops and a cherry appears. He stretches his neck from side to side and smacks another button. Another cherry appears. "Want to take the final bash?" he asks Rain.

She shakes her head.

Excitement dribbles through me at the thought of winning. I want to hit a button. But Del doesn't ask me to. He laughs and uses his fist to bang the last button really hard.

A red fruit appears and lines up with the other two. "Cherry!" Rain shouts.

I cheer and high-five Del.

"Double or nothing," he says. Without banking his winnings from the cherries, he has the slot machine whistling again.

"What are you doing? We won," I say.

"Not enough. One more go."

I bite the insides of my cheeks. Del hits the first button and a dollar sign appears. And another dollar. And a third dollar!

"No way!" I shout.

Rain yelps. The men at the other slot machines frown. Del pulls a handle by the top of the machine. Coins clink against its innards and are spewed onto a dish by our knees.

Rain collects the money. "Must be at least twenty quid there," Del says. "And I reckon that's all this machine's gonna dish out. Shall we go?"

We follow him out, find a bench on the promenade, and count. "Twenty-four pounds!" I say.

"What did I tell you?" Del blows on his fingernails and pretends to buff them on his shirt. "I should leave school and do this full-time. I'd own a Ferrari by the summer. Or, at the very least, a really cool skateboard."

Rain and I laugh. I put two pound coins in my pocket and try to hand the rest to Del. He waves me away.

"But it's yours," I say.

"I don't want it. I just like to play." He runs his hands through his hair. He smiles and I smile back.

"So, how are we going to spend it?" I ask.

"Candy!" Rain shouts.

"But not for Jenny," Del says.

Rain looks at the doll. I think she'd forgotten she was even holding her. "No. Not for Jenny."

"Okay," I say, acting like I'm indulging Rain when really the idea of a mountain of sweets sounds great. "There's a pick 'n' mix place by the pier." I point toward it.

Rain skips ahead, holding the pink teddy in one arm and Jenny in the other. Her long, scraggly braid wags like a puppy's tail.

"You don't have to hang around with us if you've got better things to do," I say to Del.

"I'll have to cancel my pedicure actually," he says. He nudges me in the side with his elbow. "So, seriously, when are you coming back to school?"

I shrug. "Wish I knew."

"You're missing out. Mr. Gaydon's got us writing gobbledygook."

"What do you mean?"

"We've been reading this poem called 'Jabberwocky' by Lewis Carroll, which has loads of made-up words in it but somehow makes sense anyway. Then we've been writing our own poems. It's sort of fun. Sort of."

I nibble at my nails. I miss English class and Mr. Gaydon's way of looking at the world. Like being ourselves is enough. "If I give you my e-mail address, can you send me a copy of the poem?" I ask Del.

"Sure thing, toots," he says.

Rain is standing outside the pick 'n' mix shop next to an old-fashioned cotton candy machine. The big wheel towers above her. "Apple, is this the place?" she shouts.

"Wait there!" I call. Then I sigh. "She's convinced that doll's real. Lately, she's been pretending it's sick. Keeps trying to get me to take her to the doctor."

My hands are swinging by my sides. So are Del's. They brush against each other. Neither of us put our hands in our pockets. "Maybe it isn't Jenny who needs a doctor, if you know what I mean," Del says.

"Mum hasn't registered her with a GP yet. It's complicated when you come from abroad."

"What I meant was, maybe Rain knows she needs a doctor and that's why she keeps asking you to take Jenny to see one."

I stop and look at him. For someone who lives on the moon, he's figured out quite a lot about the real world.

"She wants help?" I ask.

"I don't know, do I? Maybe." He pulls a packet of bubble gum from his pocket and offers me one. "Watermelon," he says. I don't like real watermelon—the texture makes me want to gag, but bubble gum's different. I take one from Del. Sweetness fills my mouth.

"If I show up at the doctor myself, they'll wonder . . ."

I trail off. I haven't told him that I'm Rain's unpaid babysitter. If I say it out loud, all the skipping school and looking after Rain might seem worse than it really is.

"Why can't your mum take her?"

"She's an actress. She's busy going to auditions and stuff."

"Right," he says like he understands, but I can see from his expression that he's trying to work something out. "So, she's acting and that means you two don't go to school?"

"Well, Rain can't go with the doll."

"Ah, right, right," he says again. He looks even more confused.

"I know what you're thinking."

"I'm not thinking anything." He pauses. "Actually, I am. I'm wondering whether a snail finds its shell heavy. I'd hate to have to carry a thing like that around."

"Stop it, Del. You think that my mum doesn't care about us. That she only cares about herself. But she needs to act to feed us and to pay the rent and . . ." I twist my hands together. The truth is I have no idea where Mum is right now or what she's doing. The only acting part she definitely has is a small role in a play and that doesn't start until next week. And then I realize she has no idea where *we* are or what we're doing either.

Would she care if she knew we'd spent the afternoon gambling on slot machines?

Del places a hand on my arm. "Are you okay?"

I feel so tired—like I might cry. Luckily Rain distracts me from my tears by jumping and waving at us.

"Hurry up!" she shouts.

"Coming!" I call. Del and I run to her.

"Right, so the price in these places is based on weight," Del tells her. "My advice is to go for the light stuff. Marshmallows, that kind of thing. Avoid Brazil nuts. Heavy as hell. Got it?"

Rain nods. "How much can I buy?"

"Hmm." Del taps his chin with his index finger. "About a third of a bag. That sound good?"

Rain nods. "Sounds great!" She looks at me and then quickly pushes Jenny into my arms and skips away. I stare at the doll. Maybe I should throw her into the nearest bin. I could tell Rain someone kidnapped her. Rain would be sad, devastated probably, but wouldn't that solve the problem? Rain could be a normal girl again, and maybe she'd like a few boys and buy makeup and feel insecure about her thighs—normal stuff like that. I suggest it to Del.

"Don't be a crazy lady. Give her here." He grabs Jenny from me and holds her on his hip like a real baby. An old man with a flat cap frowns at him, but Del doesn't care. He strokes Jenny's back. When Rain acts like Jenny's real, it gives me this sick feeling, but Del doing it makes me smile.

"What you getting?" he asks. He points at the rainbow rows of sweets snaking around the shop.

"Cola bottles," I say.

"Ah, a bit of a sweet-and-sour fan, huh? Me, I'm into black licorice."

"Ew. No one likes that."

"I do. And if you don't, it's perfect because it means you won't steal any of mine."

He grabs two paper bags. One for me. One for him. I am laughing, but I don't know why. It's not the best day of my life or the most fun, but I feel happy for the first time in ages.

And then I look at the flat paper bag and at Del and Rain picking their sweets. And I go from feeling happy to feeling like my heart is a rock. Before now I didn't even know I needed cheering up. I thought I was okay. I thought I was perfectly fine and that Rain was the one with the problem.

I load up my bag with cola bottles and realize Del was right—I'm a big sweet-and-sour fan.

34

I eat so many sweets that by the time Rain and I get home, my teeth hurt. I brush them and make Rain brush hers. Then we climb up on to her bunk with a bottle of water, a stack of books, and my laptop. I check my e-mail, and Del has already sent the poem. I read it through, and even though I don't know what all the words mean, it makes me laugh.

"What's funny?" Rain asks. She is studying a world atlas, the page open to a map of Africa.

"Just something Del sent," I tell her.

"Show me." She puts down her book.

"It's a poem called 'Jabberwocky.' I'll read a bit of it," I say. Rain leans back into her pillow to listen.

> "'*Twas brillig, and the slithy toves*
> *Did gyre and gimble in the wabe;*

All mimsy were the borogoves,
And the mome raths outgrabe."

I wiggle my fingers and tickle her tummy.

Rain giggles. "More!"

"You want me to read the whole thing?"

"With actions!" she says.

I kneel on the bed and round my back, trying to look like a monster. And I read, my voice low and growly:

"*'Beware the Jabberwock, my son!*
The jaws that bite, the claws that catch!
Beware the Jubjub bird, and shun
The frumious Bandersnatch!'"

When I've read it through to the end, Rain claps. "That *was* funny," she says. "Did Del write it?"

"No, it was someone called Lewis Carroll."

"I want to write one."

"Okay, let's," I say. I jump down from the bunk, pull my special poetry exercise book and a mechanical pencil from my bag, and climb back up next to Rain.

She is muttering to herself. "I've got the first bit," she says.

I open the book and hold the pencil ready. "Go on."

She holds a finger in the air. "She boobled down to the dirreny sonce," she says. She sounds doubtful, but I write it in the book, spelling the words however they first come to me. Rain runs her finger along the line. "What do you think it means?" she wonders.

"Hmm. I think the person is stumbling her way to a murky river."

"Yes!" Rain says. "Now your turn."

I think for a few seconds. "Alone, unarmed, her tickery jonced," I say.

Rain giggles again and taps the book. "That rhymes! Quick, write it down before you forget!"

And we do this for an hour, taking turns and discussing what the words might mean. At the end, when we read it through, we change a few of the parts so they sound creepier or so the beat of the poem goes more smoothly. And for the whole time I forget that I'm babysitting or that Rain is sick and just focus on writing something good.

"Read it from the start," Rain tells me once we've agreed it's as good as it can be.

"Why don't you?" I ask.

She twists her mouth to the side. "I'll do some actions," she says.

"Okay." I hold the book in front of me and read.

"She boobled down to the dirreny sonce
Alone, unarmed, her tickery jonced.
'What me? What my? What cooliers lie here?'
She whinnied furverly in the ghoulian ear.

And up he rose like a miney bront,
Waving his tammons and sleery flont.
'Don't wake me, don't shake me,' the ghoulian
*   gristled,*
And piped his phantons across the spistles.

A ploon bellowed out over the sheel,
And she ran as fast as her miggens could reel.
'No more dirrenies,' she whispered aloud
And slumped back down to sleep on her mound."

"Want to write another one?" I ask.

Rain shakes her head. "I'm going to pee," she says. She scuttles down the ladder.

I jiggle the pencil, and the spare lead quietly ticks against the plastic casing. I want to write my own poem now. Another nonsense poem, or maybe two or three of them. And so I do. I write until it's dark outside. Until Rain has finished studying her atlas and until Mum calls from the kitchen to tell us she's finally home.

35

Mum is so tired from working all week that she sleeps late on Saturday. She appears at noon and collapses on the couch. She watches TV and sips coffee, both hands hugging the mug. When Rain takes a shower, I make myself tea and sit next to her. I turn off the TV.

Mum's eyebrows knit together. "I'm so grateful for everything you're doing, Apple. You load and unload the dishwasher, you keep on top of all the laundry and grocery shopping. I don't know what I'd do without you. I don't know what I ever did." She goes back to her coffee. "But I promise you I'm close to getting a babysitter. I'm so close."

"We have to talk about Rain," I say. I know I sound a bit serious; I need her to listen and do something.

"Oh, please don't tell me she's too much for you. I couldn't take it." She presses her fingertips against her temples.

"She really has to see a doctor. I think she *wants* to see a doctor."

"I've already told you that Doctor Bronson in Brooklyn said—"

I cut her off. "I know what he said. But that was months ago, and Rain's no better. She's worse. She keeps pretending Jenny's on death's door."

"If only." Mum shakes her head.

"I don't think she can help it," I say.

Mum scratches her head. "I keep hoping it will go away on its own. I thought that if she had a sister, she'd stop all this nonsense."

"What do you mean?"

"Well, I always wanted to come back to England, but once Rain got sick and started obsessing about that stupid doll, I knew it was time. I needed help raising her, so I had to come back. For Rain, if not for myself."

I stare at the rings of tea stains in my mug. I don't know what to say—I feel like someone is pouring dirty old sludge into me.

Mum quickly realizes what she's said and throws herself at me. "Oh God, Apple, I know what that sounds like, but I came back for you too. I missed you so much."

She cradles my head in her arms, but it hurts my neck. I push her away and sit up straight. "Why did you leave in the first place?" I ask. It's what I've lived all my life wondering and been too afraid to ask until now: Why did Mum leave? Was I that unlovable?

Mum goes to the window and lights a cigarette.

"It wasn't about you," she says.

"But you left me behind. Why couldn't you have taken me with you?" I ask.

"How could I care for you? I couldn't even take care of myself."

"Then you should've stayed. Nana would have cared for both of us," I say.

"Your grandmother threw me out, Apple. If you want the truth, then that's it. Your perfect, oh-so-virtuous, religious grandmother kicked me out." She drags on the cigarette like it'll be her last breath. "What should I have done? Brought you with me? I didn't have a job, and I had no money. I wanted to be an actress. It was no life for a baby."

When Nana tells the story of Mum leaving, she skips the bit about her kicking Mum out. She pretends it was all Mum's doing. But that means the story I have in my head about what happened the night Mum left isn't true either—it means I've made the whole thing up. Mum never rushed out, Nana pleading with her to stay—Nana pushed Mum out into the storm.

"*Mom*, there's no shampoo and my hair's like an old greaseball!" Rain is standing in a towel and dripping all over the carpet.

Mum stubs out her cigarette. She throws the butt out of the window without looking to see where it will land. "I'll go and get some today. I'm really sorry." She does sound sorry, but I don't think she cares that much about shampoo. "If you dry your hair quickly we can all go to Pizza Express for lunch." She looks at me meaningfully, but I don't know why. And I don't think she really knows why either. But Pizza Express is a start—it's better than sitting around drinking coffee and watching TV all day long.

"Dough balls!" Rain shouts. She turns and drops the towel before she reaches our room so that her naked bum is the last thing I see of her. I laugh. Mum looks up, a bit relieved to see I'm not grumpy anymore.

"You remind me of your grandmother sometimes," she says.

"Oh," I say.

"No, no. In a good way. You're firm but fair. Like a strict teacher. You know?"

I shrug. I don't want to be like a strict teacher—that's her job.

"Mum . . ."

"Yes?"

"Who is Rain's dad?"

Mum shakes her head. "Oh, just some loser. Never should have gone near him."

"Was Dad a loser too?"

Mum laughs.

"I'm serious."

She chews on her knuckles. "Your dad was lovely. But we were both young. It wouldn't have worked between us. I see him now and I know it *definitely* wouldn't have worked."

"You gave me a stupid long Greek name."

"I wanted you to have a history, Apple. And back then, well, I loved your dad." This could be true. I know that how Mum acts isn't always how she feels. "Have you seen this?" she says. She pushes the band of her tracksuit bottoms down a fraction. There's a green mark on her hip.

"What is it?" I ask.

She steps closer so I can see. It's a tattoo. But not any old tattoo. It's an apple. A tiny, bright-green apple, hidden from the world but permanently and secretly stamped on Mum's skin. "You were always with me, honey," she says. "Look, I know you're upset, but it was a long time ago that I left. Can't you forgive me? I'm back and I'm *trying*."

I hug her. She has me tattooed on her skin—she loves me that much.

And she's right. It *was* all a long time ago. People change. Everyone deserves a second chance.

36

After we're stuffed from too much pizza and ice cream, Mum takes us to the park to feed the ducks. The sun's come out a bit. The tree leaves are beginning to bud. Ducks jostle for the scraps of pizza crust we throw into the water. Rain makes quacking sounds until a mallard takes a fancy to her and follows her around the pond. We laugh and laugh, and I start thinking this is the beginning of it all—the beginning of us acting like a real family—until Mum's phone rings and she rushes off to answer it in secret.

Rain stops quacking and throws the rest of the crust she's holding on the ground.

"Want to play on the swings?" I ask her. I don't want the phone call to mean anything, and if I can convince Rain everything is fine, maybe it will be.

"Nope," she says. She finds a bench and sits on it. I

plonk myself next to her and wait for Mum. I thrash my legs violently whenever a duck gets too close. They're cute when you're throwing food at them, but when they're surrounding you and pecking at your feet, it's sort of horrifying.

After ten minutes, Mum steps out from behind an oak tree. She sits between us on the bench.

"I've got to go to London tomorrow afternoon for an audition. It's an American casting director I met in New York. He's in London for the weekend. This could be a big break for me. I know it's a huge thing to ask, Apple, but could you be in charge until I get back on Monday morning?"

I lash out at a duck and almost kick it in the head. It spits at me and waddles away. Mum titters. I don't. And neither does Rain.

"You'll be gone overnight?" After everything we talked about this morning and after the fun we've had this afternoon, I thought things might change. I so badly wanted it to be different from how it was. I wanted everything to be better.

"I know what you're thinking, but I'll get an early train and be back home by eight. You won't miss another school day."

But Mum's got it all wrong. I don't care about school. I just want *her* to care about me going to school like any other normal mother.

"Can't you get a late train home on Sunday evening instead?" I ask.

"Roles go to the people who have time to schmooze, and that can mean cavorting into the early hours. It's a petty business." She squeezes my knee. "Apple, I *promise* this is the last time you'll have to do this. I've spoken to Gina, and she's going to pop in to make sure you're all right. She's going to help with the weekdays from now on too. Okay? Please say it's okay. *Please*." Her face is a picture of worry, and I don't want to be the reason for it. I want her to be happy. I want everyone to be happy.

"You should go to London," I say because part of me wants to believe it really will be the last time and that if I say yes, everything will be better.

But a bigger part of me knows it won't be any different after Monday. It won't be any different at all.

37

Mum leaves early Sunday afternoon, once Rain and I are back from Mass and a cup of tea at Nana's. I warn Rain not to tell Nana that Mum is staying away overnight. She promises not to say a word, but I get nervous that maybe *I'll* let it slip, so I make an excuse as soon as we've had our tea and rush home, leaving Nana to eat Sunday dinner alone and probably feed most of the stew she's cooked to Derry.

Mum makes us peanut butter and jam sandwiches for dinner and has stocked up on Coco Pops and yogurts. "You've got food, money, and my number. And remember not to open the door . . . unless it's Gina."

"How will we know it's Gina?" Rain asks. It's the first time she's spoken to Mum since the park.

"*Ask*," Mum snaps. Then she remembers herself. "Right, so be good. I love you both, and I'll see you in less than twenty-four hours. Cross your fingers and toes for me."

"Good luck," I manage to say.

She is wearing a short red dress, puffy at the sleeves with lace across the back. Her hair is backcombed so it looks a bit like a wasp's nest. She doesn't look bad exactly, but she doesn't look like she's going to find work, that's all. She clip-clops down the stairs in her high heels.

"What about your coat?" I call after her.

"Coats are for cowards," she shouts back.

And she's out the door.

I look at Rain. Rain looks at me.

"The library's closed," I say.

"And no good films on TV until after seven o'clock."

"We could read," I suggest.

Rain shakes her head. "I've finished all my books. I'd have to read one of yours, and I think they're all about kissing."

"They are," I admit.

"Ugh." She pauses to caress one of Jenny's hands. "We could knock for Del and ask him to take us to the slots again. That was fun."

"It was," I say. "Let's do that."

*　*　*

Del opens the door before I knock. He's got beads in his hair and I think he's wearing black eyeliner. He's swapped his rain shoes for heavy boots with the laces undone.

"I had a hunch it would be you two," he says. He hitches up his jeans, which are hanging, crumpled and loose, on his waist.

"How?" Rain asks. She is beaming at him like someone in love. But she's ten. She can't be in love. Can she?

"I've got spidey-sense, which is weird because I'm actually Batman," he says.

"He's got binoculars," I tell Rain, and point at the pair hanging around his neck. "Who have you been spying on?"

"Let's just say, I might have seen two bare bums today . . . So, what's the plan? Bit of ballroom dancing followed by some carjacking, topped off with a dash of fly-fishing?"

"I hate fish," Rain says. "Especially octopuses."

"We could always go ice skating and do the fishing and other stuff another day. What do you think?" Del asks.

"I think yes," Rain says.

"You're bankrolling this operation, I hope," he says,

looking at me. I smile. I can't help it because when Del looks at me he really looks at me, never at my legs or hair or anything else. He sees through all that stuff.

"I've got loads of money," I say.

And we head off to the ice rink.

*　　*　　*

It's only once we've put on our skates and wobbled across the rubber mats to the rink that Rain wonders whether ice skating might be dangerous while she's carrying Jenny.

"Could be. You want me to watch her while you two take a few laps?" Del asks.

Rain shakes her head. "I want us to go on together."

"I saw a babysitting service on our way in. We could leave Jenny there to play with the other babies, if you think she'd like that," I say. I don't expect her to agree, but after considering it for a few seconds, she nods.

"Great! I'll be back in a minute," I say. I take Jenny from her and head for the babysitting area. But if I show up with Jenny they'll think I'm as loopy as Rain—loopier. Besides, why would I waste three pounds leaving her there when I could stuff her into my locker for free? Rain need never know.

I almost have to fold Jenny in two and twist her head right around to make her fit in my locker, but eventually I manage to get the door closed. I'm so used to acting like Jenny's real, I feel a bit bad leaving her.

When I get back to the rink, Del is leading Rain onto the ice. She looks like she's about to slip. Even so, she is smiling.

"Was Jenny okay when you left?" she asks.

"She was perfect," I say. I try not to think how bent out of shape Jenny looked when I closed the locker.

"Come on. Let's fall over and soak ourselves silly on the ice!" Del says.

And that's exactly what Rain and I do. But Del is an ice skating pro. He zips across the rink like he's powered by gasoline, weaving in and out of wobbling skaters and dodging small clusters of children. And he can go backward.

I've only been ice skating once before, so within an hour the knees of my jeans are wet. But I don't care. I shuffle around the rink without hanging on to the barrier, sometimes even gliding a bit, and whenever I fall, Del cheers, which makes me laugh so hard I can barely stand up. He grabs my hand a few times and pulls me along fast. I scream, but not seriously. And he leads Rain along too, helping her keep her balance and showing her how best to fall over, so she won't hurt herself.

Once our legs start to burn, we leave the ice. "I'll get Jenny," Rain says. She heads for the babysitting area.

I jump in front of her. "No, no. Here." I hand her some money. "You buy the Fanta and chips . . . I mean french fries . . . and I'll meet you upstairs."

"I want to see the babysitting service," Rain says.

I give Del a long look, and he understands. "Rain, *help* me!" he calls out. He lumbers up the rubber stairs to the café, still wearing his skates. He grins and flails his arms like he's about to fall. Rain giggles and totters up the stairs after him. I sneak off to the lockers where I retrieve Jenny.

"Sorry I left you all squished up in there. Come on, let's go and find Mummy," I say aloud. I hold Jenny close.

Then I hear a snigger. I go rigid.

When I turn around, Pilar and Donna are watching me.

"I've heard of Doctor Dolittle talking to the animals, but who are you supposed to be?" Donna says. She nudges Pilar, who laughs nervously.

"Apple?" Pilar says. She looks genuinely worried, like I might actually have fallen off my rocker. I want to say something, but how can I explain talking to a plastic doll? Pilar doesn't know Rain exists, and even if she did, I still couldn't really explain Jenny to her.

"Is that why you haven't been at school? Have you been caring for your baby all day?" Donna laughs.

My throat closes up. My eyes well with tears. Donna thinks she's really funny. She can't know how close to the truth she is. "My sister . . . ," I mutter, thinking that an explanation might make sense after all.

"She's your sister? Ah, that's lovely. Did your nan have her?" Donna is doubled over laughing. She tries to prod Jenny, but I pull away to keep the doll out of her reach.

"Honestly, Pilar, you told me Apple was a bit immature, but you never said she still played with dolls. I mean, that's so abnormal. Come on, let's go." With a titter, Donna struts off.

Pilar stays where she is. "What's going on, Apple?" she asks.

I wish I could tell her everything that's been happening. She's supposed to be my best friend. We used to share our biggest secrets with each other. But I can't trust her anymore, so I let myself cry and eventually Pilar slogs after Donna like a well-trained dog.

In the café, Del and Rain are sitting by a glass window overlooking the rink. Del is doing impressions of animals, and Rain is screeching.

"Your fries are getting cold," he says.

"I don't care. We have to go home. Now."

"I thought we'd take another turn around the pond before spring arrives," Del says, trying to be funny as usual. But none of this is funny. Not Mum going away overnight and leaving me to take care of Rain, and certainly not Rain's weird belief that Jenny's got a soul. I don't know why I've been spending time with Del messing around instead of facing up to my life. It's getting me nowhere.

"Can we go, *please*?" I say. I practically throw Jenny at Rain and march off down the stairs, trying not to fall over in my skates.

"Wait up!" Del runs after me. "What's wrong? What's happened?"

"I don't want to do any more of this, that's what's happened. I just saw Pilar and Donna from school, who thought that me talking to a doll was hil*a*rious. And then I realized, it isn't hilarious at all. If I was a bit gutsier I would have told my mum that a long time ago. But I didn't. And do you want to know why I didn't?"

Del stares.

"Because I wanted my mum to think I was cool. How sad is *that*?"

"I dunno, I mean . . ."

Rain has caught up with us. Her mouth is covered in ketchup. "Can't we stay for a few more minutes?" she asks.

"Apple's a bit upset," Del says.

"Yes, I am. And you know who I'm upset with? Myself, that's who, because to win Mum over I kicked Nana aside, even though she's loved me nonstop for fourteen years. And maybe she is strict, but she cares. And it's more than I did. I've made a mess of every-thing. *Everything.*"

Del nods like he understands. But how could he? He lives with his hippie mum and dad who buy him frog sweaters and eat seeds for Christmas dinner. "You know what you need, Apple?" he says. He takes my hand and pinches it lightly.

"A bit of wine added to my Coke to help my nerves?" I ask. "Have you ever had a calimocho? I can make you one. I couldn't before, but I can now."

He shakes his head. He doesn't look impressed. "I'm actually serious for once. You need to go home and get

268

some sleep. My mum always says a new day shines a bright light on a dark problem."

"I'm so tired," I say.

"I know. Come on, let's go home," he says.

We unlace the skates and swap them for our shoes. I spot Donna and Pilar heading for the ice, arm in arm like proper best friends. I turn away so they won't know I've seen them—so they can't show off how happy they are together.

Del waits at the bus stop then waves us off. The bus shudders up the hill toward home. When we get there, a note from Gina is pinned to the front door: *I called when you were out. Any probs, I'm working at the Hungry Horse until midnight.*

So much for keeping an eye on us. I rip the note into small pieces and throw it behind me onto the shared porch.

*   *   *

We're watching a Discovery program about polar bears when Rain slides closer to me and tucks her bare feet under my legs.

"It's me," she says.

"What?"

269

"Mom would be happy if I was never born. She went to America to be an actress, but then I came along and ruined everything. I'm still ruining everything." She pauses. Her voice is as fragile as a ladybug's wing.

"Mum's busy, Rain. I'd hate a lazy mum, wouldn't you?" I say.

"I guess," Rain says. She lifts Jenny's bum to her nose and sniffs. "Poop," she says.

"Oh, Rain." I groan.

"What?" she asks. She screws up her face and squeals as though she really can smell poo.

"Nothing," I say.

Because what *can* I say? She's totally round the bend.

38

I make breakfast with the last dribble of milk, which is past its sell-by date but smells okay. And after breakfast I clear up. Rain tucks into *Charlie and the Chocolate Factory* and a carton of apple juice.

"What time did Mom say she'd be home?" Rain asks. She turns a page in her book.

"Don't remember," I lie. It's already nine o'clock and she said she'd be back by eight.

I'm about to go and get my own reading book when the doorbell jangles.

"That's her," Rain says.

"She's got a key," I say.

I pad down the stairs and through the porch. I slide the security chain into place then open the main door and peer out.

I don't believe it. Standing there grinning is my English teacher.

271

"Mr. Gaydon?"

"Hello, Apple. I heard from the office that you were visiting your dad. But I see you're back."

I nod slowly, wondering how I'm going to lie my way out of this.

"Is your mother at home?"

"She's, uh, she's . . ." If I say Mum isn't here he might think I'm being neglected. If I say Mum *is* here he'll want to speak to her. Either way, I'm stuck.

"Who is it?" Rain shouts from upstairs.

Mr. Gaydon pokes the security chain with his finger. "Can I come in?"

I unchain the door but stand in the frame so he can't get by. "Mum's not well. Can you come back later?"

"You know you're racking up a lot of unauthorized absences, and I think I might know why. I have to speak to your mum about it." He taps his foot noiselessly.

"Mum's in bed, and I'm taking care of her," I say.

"And who's taking care of you?"

"Is it Gina?" Rain shouts down again. My heart pounds. She doesn't sound like an adult, but maybe the American accent will fool Mr. Gaydon.

"That's my mum," I say. "You see, I got the flu and then she caught it from me."

Mr. Gaydon wrinkles his nose. "And you were never in London with your dad?"

"No, sir. I don't know who said I was."

He sighs. "Apple, I checked your record and you've had sixteen unauthorized absences after a previously pristine record. I know you're having some problems with girls in your class. I think we all need to sit down and discuss what's going on. I think I need to speak to Donna's and Pilar's parents too."

"Don't do that! I'm fine. I'm coming back in today . . . Later." I put a pleading hand on Mr. Gaydon's arm. He steps back.

"I need to see your mother. If I don't, this will have to go further." Maybe he means he'll tell Dr. Dillon. But he could mean social services or the police. Could Mum be arrested for not sending Rain and me to school?

"Mum's sick, sir," I repeat.

"Are you sick?"

"No, sir."

"Good. So, run up the stairs and put your uniform on. My car's parked around the corner."

"Mum needs someone to take care of her. But I'll definitely be in school tomorrow."

"And what have you been doing at home for two

weeks? You've missed a lot of work. I thought you liked poetry."

"I do."

Mr. Gaydon bites his thumbnail. "Look, let's make a deal. You come to school this week, or I'll be back here with the cavalry." He pauses. "Do you know what that means?"

"You'll bring other people?"

"An army of people."

"Yes, sir."

"And I'll expect you to e-mail me one hundred words in response to this poem." He pulls a piece of paper from his briefcase and hands it to me.

"What's the poem about?"

"Blackberries," he says. "It's also about much more. It's your job to work out what that is. And don't cheat by going online."

"Thank you, sir."

"See you *soon*," he says.

I race up the stairs. Rain peeks over the rim of her book. "Was it Gina?" she asks.

"Mum had better get back soon," I say.

"Why?" Rain goes to the window. "Who's that man?"

"He's a teacher. He wants to speak to Mum about me not being in school."

"Oh."

Is that all she can say? Oh? She doesn't seem to realize this is serious. Children can't just skip school. It's illegal. And it's not as though any of this is an accident either. It's *her* fault I've not been going in. If she acted more like a normal human being, I wouldn't have to babysit every day.

"We *both* have to go back to school, Rain," I say.

"We will," she replies. "Soon."

39

By noon, Mum's still not home. I try her phone again and again but it's switched off. For lunch I make more breakfast because we've run out of cash. Rain complains that it's too lumpy, so I go and check the mail to stop myself from throwing the bowls against the wall. Then I make us two mugs of tea and sit at the dining table tackling Mr. Gaydon's assignment. The poem is called "Blackberry-Picking" by someone called Seamus Heaney, and it's basically about people who pick ripe blackberries and fill a bath with them. They try to keep the berries fresh but it's impossible and eventually the whole lot rots and the narrator feels fed up about it.

I read through it a couple of times, then look up the words I don't understand in an online dictionary. I think it might help me analyze the poem better. It doesn't make a difference; even though Mr. Gaydon said the poem was about more than blackberries, I can't work out the underlying message.

Rain sits next to me. She grabs the poem and reads it aloud very slowly. "Are you learning about fruit?" she asks.

"Poems," I say.

"Poems are boring."

"But you liked writing the nonsense poem."

"Yeah, but that wasn't a real poem. That was silly."

"Poems are good if you think about them a bit like a puzzle. You have to pick all the words apart until you understand the meaning," I tell her.

"Well, I can tell that the meaning of this one is bad. Whatever it is, it's a very bad meaning," she says.

"How can you tell?"

"I don't know. A feeling."

"A feeling?"

"Yeah. Anyway, there's all bad words in it like 'rat' and 'stinking.' It's yucky."

I read the poem over again in my head. Rain's right. The poem is gloomy, especially at the end where the blackberries get all gray and moldy. It's sad because the person tries to save the berries but they get ruined anyway.

And the worst part about it is, he does the same thing every year and never seems to learn his lesson.

I tap my teeth with my fingernails, thinking. Rain opens the freezer and takes out an orange Popsicle. She goes back to reading.

I go back to the laptop.

"Disappointment" by Apple Apostolopoulou

All the time Mum was away,
Eleven long years,
I saved up my hopes
Like little pennies in a jar.
I didn't know her, so I made her up—
And I made her perfect.
In my mind, Mum shimmered like the moon against
*   the sea—*
Ghostly and romantic.
But now I know that
She is scratched and stained
And all that's left is disappointment.

I thought when she came back
I'd have everything that was missing

278

From my life.
Now all I have
Is an empty jar with
A hole in the bottom to stop
New hopes from heaping up.

For the first time, I don't write another one hundred words for Mr. Gaydon. Instead, I write him an e-mail.

Dear Mr. Gaydon,

I am attaching my homework. I think the poem by Seamus Heaney is very sad. It seems to be about how we try to hold on to things that cannot be captured, like fresh fruit. Seamus Heaney uses this as a metaphor for life, and it made me think about my mum. When I was a small child, I thought she was perfect. Actually, until a few days ago I still thought she was the coolest person in the world. Now I know she's just normal and makes mistakes. So, that's why I wrote a poem called "Disappointment" about her. I hope it's okay. I know that sometimes you like us to read our work out loud in class, but this poem is personal, so please don't make me read it to anyone when I get back.

Thank you,

Apple Apostolopoulou

I press Send, then spend five minutes with my head in my hands, wishing I'd written a fake answer. I hardly know Mr. Gaydon. Maybe he's one of those teachers who gossips about students in the staff room. By the time I go back to school, the poem could be halfway around the building.

I sit up straight only when my computer pings with a new message. It's from Mr. Gaydon.

Dear Apple,

I just read your poem. I don't want to give you a big head, but let me tell you that I've now read two of your poems and I don't think their excellence is a fluke. I think, perhaps, you have talent. But as with all talents, it must be nurtured. Have you been using the book I gave you to write other poems? Perhaps you'll e-mail them to me?

I have attached a copy of an extract from a poem by Rupert Brooke called "The Great Lover," which we read in class today. Your homework is to write about things you love using this poem as a template. I'm sure you'll do a wonderful job. Good luck!

Mr. G

I gape at the screen. I don't think a teacher has ever told me I'm talented, not even Mr. Rowls who proclaims that everyone, even the percussion players, have "musical gifts." I open my poetry exercise book and flick through its pages. I must have written ten or fifteen poems already, and loads of other unfinished snippets. I hardly even noticed myself doing it.

I open a fresh Word document on my laptop and start to type up some of the poems. As I do, I end up changing them. Not to make them less real but to make them better, to add in some alliteration or rhyme or dramatic punctuation. And then I write Mr. Gaydon another e-mail. I type quickly.

Dear Mr. Gaydon,

I don't know whether or not I have talent, but as I've been off school for a while, I've had time to write more poems. I have included them with this e-mail, so you can see that I've not been lazy and that I like English.

Thank you,

Apple

I press Send. Most of my poems are about Mum or Nana or Rain, and a trickle of fear runs through me as I wonder what Mr. Gaydon will do with the poems. He could forward them to anyone he wanted. He could forward them to our school's child protection officer.

I'm too jittery to read or write anymore so I sit by the window waiting for Mum—watching. Every car that pulls up makes my heart race. Every click-clacking pair of shoes makes me crane forward to see who it is.

Then I start imagining Mum lying in a hospital bed after being attacked on the train or laid out on a slab of concrete, dead, because someone's stabbed her. I can hardly keep the horrible thoughts from rolling in.

"Where *is* she?" I say aloud.

"Maybe she went back to America and left us both here," Rain says. She turns a page in her book.

"That's not funny."

"Wasn't a joke."

A motorbike revs its engine. I watch it drive by.

Would Mum do something like that? Would she book a ticket to New York and leave us to fend for ourselves? She knows Nana would show up eventually. And maybe that's her plan. Maybe it was her plan all along—to force Rain and me together and when she knew we were okay, dump us.

"She'll be here any second. Let's stay calm," I suggest.

"I am calm," Rain replies. She has almost finished the Roald Dahl book. "But if she doesn't come back, can I stay with you?" she asks.

"She'll come back," I say. She has to come back.

40

When seven o'clock arrives, I've convinced myself that Mum is in Brooklyn. But instead of dwelling on it, I keep busy. I make more oatmeal, this time with water because we're out of milk. Rain won't eat it. She finds half a cucumber to chew on instead. We sit opposite each other at the dining table, miserable and hungry.

"We need money," Rain says.

"I know," I say. My stomach rumbles, and I look in the fridge again. There's an onion, two beers, and a knob of butter. I take out one of the beers and open it. It tastes a bit like dirt, but it's cold and fizzy and better than the oatmeal. I pour it into a clean glass.

"I don't mind cucumber, but Jenny needs formula," Rain says. Jenny is propped on her knee. She pats the doll's head.

She still thinks that the flour she's been using, and that I've been restocking, is formula.

"Jenny's in good shape," I say.

"I know. I'm only saying that in the morning we'll need milk or formula. Right?"

"Give it a rest, Rain."

"Why should I give it a rest?"

I rub my forehead. "I have enough to worry about, don't you think?"

"Just because you don't care about Jenny doesn't mean I shouldn't."

I stare at her, unbelieving. All day she's had her head in a book and hardly bothered about the doll. Jenny probably had her diaper changed once since breakfast and none of us have been for a walk. But suddenly Jenny's hungry and we all need to rally around taking care of her.

"Get real," I say. I take another sip of beer.

Rain won't give it up. "What do you mean, get real?"

I glare at her. "What do I *mean*? Well, in case you haven't noticed, Mum's missing, the school is on my back, we have no money for food or drink, and your only concern is for Jenny."

"She's a baby."

"Is she, Rain?" I ask.

"Yes, she is. She's my baby."

I roll my eyes. I can't help it. Rain's delusion is too

much on top of everything. "You're ten years old. When exactly did you have her?" I ask.

"Jenny's my baby," Rain mutters.

I lower my voice. "No. She. Isn't. You know she's a doll. Don't you?"

She holds up Jenny for my inspection. "She isn't some doll," Rain says.

I grab Jenny and pull her to my face. I sniff her. "She smells like plastic, Rain," I say. And then I shake her. Hard.

Rain gasps.

"She doesn't *sound* like a real baby either. Not a murmur."

"Give her back," Rain groans.

"Do you think she feels what a real baby feels?" I ask.

Rain stares at me, frightened. "Don't hurt her," she says.

"I couldn't if I tried. Can't you see that she isn't real? She isn't *real*," I say.

Rain tries to snatch Jenny back. I hold the doll above my head.

"Stop," Rain pleads.

But I can't stop. I won't. Rain needs to hear the truth. It'll make everything easier for everyone.

I release my grip on Jenny, and she drops to the floor.

Rain starts to cry. And then I'm crying too. I look down at Jenny and, without thinking, kick her across the room. Jenny hits the wall and slides to the ground.

"Jenny!" Rain shrieks.

I move toward them. "Keep away from us! I hate you. I hate you, I hate you." Rain can hardly breathe.

I can't believe what I've done. "I'm so sorry," I manage. And I am. Rain didn't deserve it. And neither did Jenny.

I drop the beer bottle.

"You're a *monster*!" Rain shouts. She dashes into our bedroom with Jenny in her arms. "I wish you'd never come to live here. I wish you were dead!"

"Rain, wait," I say. No one's ever hated me before. Not with such fire and pain. But I don't go after her. I don't know what to say. I can't take back what I've done. And she'd be right never to speak to me again. As far as she's concerned, I've tried to kill her child.

I slump onto the floor. Where is Mum, and why isn't she here to make sure nothing terrible like this happens? That's her job—to take care of us and help us take care of each other. I want to call and leave a long, nasty message on her cell phone. But I'm sobbing too hard to speak.

41

It's dark when I wake. I glance at the display on the microwave—it's five o'clock in the morning. I pull myself off the couch and run down to Mum's bedroom. I push open her door. The room is empty. The duvet is untidily piled at the end of her bed where she left it. "Mum?" I say aloud. But it's pointless. She's not here.

I sigh and go into my own room. I lie on my bunk in the dark, hugging a pillow.

"Rain?" I want her to talk to me or even shout at me. I don't want to be alone. But if she can hear me, she doesn't answer. She doesn't move a muscle. And it's so quiet in the room I think that maybe she's holding her breath. "Rain."

I stand on my tiptoes and scan the top bunk. Jenny is lying naked across the pillow. I pull back the duvet, expecting to find Rain tucked into the bottom corner.

The bunk's empty.

"Rain," I say again.

She wasn't in Mum's room or in the bathroom when I walked by. I look again in both rooms anyway, turning on as many lights as I can.

"RAIN!" I shout.

I dash into the sitting room, and search every tiny space. Behind the couch. In the cupboards. Under the chairs.

But I can't find her. I can't find her because she's gone, along with her coat and boots.

And the most frightening thing about it: she's left Jenny behind.

42

I call Mum again and again and again, but every time I do, it goes straight to voice mail. I've no choice but to stick a note on the front door for Rain, telling her to call me if she gets back before I do, and I head out to search for her. I jam Jenny into a dress, strap her into the carrier, and bring her with me. I can't leave her in the flat alone—not after what I've done.

I close the front door behind me and pull up the hood of my coat. The streets are deserted, and all I want to do is go back inside. I want to hide and pretend none of this is happening. But I can't do that with Rain missing. Not after she was so upset. And especially not when it's my fault.

I turn right at the end of the road then left onto the high street. The shops are closed, the shutters down. Homeless people in sleeping bags are curled up in cold doorways. A van rattles along the road, stops outside the newsagent's, and a man throws a bundle of newspapers by the door. The bakery is dimly lit, and a smell of fresh bread wafts its way onto the street.

I trek up and down the high street three times. But Rain is not here. I don't know why I thought she might be.

A woman in white dungarees is fiddling with a key in the lock of a car door. She sees me and stares. "You all right, love?" she asks. She coughs and drinks from a thermos.

"Have you seen a little girl with curly red hair?" I ask.

"Is someone lost? Do your parents know you're out in the dark?"

I swallow. "Yes, of course. My sister is missing. Mum and Dad have gone to the police station," I lie. And as I say it, I know that's exactly where I should be: at the police station filing a missing person's report, not jeopardizing Rain's safety by searching myself. Then I think about Mum and what would happen to her if the police got involved, and I know I can't go anywhere near the station. Not yet. I just have to look harder.

"Thanks anyway," I tell the woman and take off down the high street toward the pier.

I hear the ocean before I see it—the heavy sound of the night waves roiling against the sand. I walk along the pier, and it creaks under my feet. Gulls circle the navy sky. It's still too dark to see along the full length of it. Water growls against its bones.

A few meters ahead is the silhouette of a man in a rain jacket. The figure turns my way. "Hello?" he calls.

My hands sweat. My heart pounds. I walk toward him.

As I get closer, I see he has a fishing rod propped up against a bucket and a line dripping into the sea.

"I'm looking for a little girl," I tell him.

"Not seen no one," he says. His face is in shadow.

I turn and head back to the promenade.

"What's her name?" he calls after me.

I ignore him and check my phone for the hundredth time to see if Mum or Rain has called. They haven't, and it's six thirty already. It means Rain has been missing well over an hour at least. I put my arms around Jenny. I don't think I've ever felt so alone.

But I might have one friend I can call on for help.

Then I'll have to go and see Nana with the terrible news.

43

I ping pebbles at the top-story windows of Del's house. After a few seconds he pushes one open. "Hey there!" he says casually, like he was expecting me.

"I need your help," I whisper.

Del opens the front door a few minutes later. He's fully dressed in his school uniform and carrying his mermaid bag.

"You're ready for school? That was quick," I say.

"Not really. Sometimes I sleep in my uniform, to save time."

I can't tell whether he's joking or not, but I'm not in the mood to quiz him. "Oh, Del, I kicked Jenny," I tell him.

"Where's Rain?" he asks.

"I *kicked* Jenny across the room. Rain's run away, and I keep thinking she must have jumped off the pier or fallen in front of a train or been kidnapped or something."

Del chews his lips. "Did your mum call the police?"

"No," I say. I hold my head in my hands. "Mum's not been home in two days. She went to London to try to get some part in a film and we haven't heard from her. She's missing too. And I'm too scared to go to the police. What if they arrest Mum for neglect or something?"

We sit on his front wall. The sun is turning the sky into a pastel-orange paste.

"Look, we'll find her. And you can't blame yourself. Rain's fragile," Del says.

"I know she's fragile. So why did I kick her doll? I'm a terrible person."

"No, you're not. *I* like you, and I hate terrible people," Del says. "If you weren't so upset and Rain wasn't missing, I'd try to kiss you. Like on the lips."

I stare at him. Kiss me? I've no makeup on and I'm dressed in a dirty sweater. My face is red from crying, and my eyes are probably bloodshot with bags underneath them.

"Don't seem so surprised," he says. "You're quite kissable. But enough of that. Let's work out where Rain is."

"Oh God, I hope she's alive. What if she isn't?"

"Let's work on the assumption that she is. Right, so who does she know in Brampton-on-Sea?"

"Jenny," I say unhelpfully.

"Jenny. Yes. Who else?"

"You?"

Del nods. "Well, *I* haven't seen her."

"I looked everywhere I could think of. She doesn't know Brampton at all, and she doesn't know anyone except us."

"Are you sure?"

I think for a second. "Well, she knows Nana, but if she'd turned up there, Nana would have called. She wouldn't hide her and not tell anyone. She's very responsible."

"Good point. So, in conclusion, she knows no one and has nowhere to go. What would you do if you were her?"

"Kill myself," I say.

"Well, that's just silly, she didn't do that. She's somewhere. We simply have to find her. Who do you know with a car?"

"No one."

"No one?"

"Nana, but I can't ask her. I can't tell her yet."

We sit in silence. The only other person I know with a car is Egan Winters, and I'm pretty sure he thinks I'm the stupidest person alive. He'd never help.

"You know someone," Del says, reading me.

"I don't," I say.

"Not to be dramatic or anything, but Rain's safety sort of depends on us finding her."

"Well, there's this senior boy with a car, but . . ."

"Where does he live?"

"I don't know."

"Right." He looks at his watch. "It's only seven fifteen. Let's retrace your steps to make sure you didn't miss anything, pick up a couple of croissants for breakfast, then go to school and wait for him." He jumps up. "You coming or what?"

"I can't ask him to drive us around. It's complicated," I say.

His mouth slips into a smile. "What? Were you *lovers* or something?" He kisses his own hand, biting and sucking the skin. It's kind of disgusting but also quite funny.

"Stop," I say, laughing, and because I'm laughing it means I don't have to explain why it's complicated with Egan Winters. Anyway, Del's right. It isn't complicated. Not at all. It's just really, really embarrassing.

295

He takes my arm, and we go the long way to the bakery for breakfast, where Del buys me an almond croissant. Then we head to school to wait for Egan.

*　　*　　*

Egan scuffs his hubcaps against the curb and clambers out of his car. "All right, Egan!" Del says, like they've been friends for years.

"Who are you?" Egan is suspicious. Then he sees me. "Apple. Hey. I thought you'd left school. Everyone thought you'd gone to America with . . ." He doesn't finish his sentence because he doesn't want to mention my mum.

"Remember my sister?" I ask.

"No," he says.

"Well, she's missing," I say.

And I tell him everything about Rain and Jenny, and about Mum leaving us and going to London. "Basically, I don't know anyone with a car except you. Can you help us find her?"

He shifts his weight from one foot to the other. He checks his phone. It's obvious he wants nothing to do with this, but he owes me a favor after humiliating me. "I've gotta be back for orchestra," he says.

"Great. Come on," says Del.

We pile into Egan's Punto, which smells a bit like cheese-and-onion chips. Del jumps into the back. I sit next to Egan in the passenger seat.

Egan stalls the car a couple of times before pulling away.

"When did you pass your test?" Del asks. He pokes his head between the seats.

"It's a sticky gearbox," Egan says to explain his bad driving.

"Ah," Del says. "Anyway, the best way to do this is if Egan drives and we hop out to look. That'll save us time trying to find parking and whatever."

"Seat belt," Egan barks.

Del sits back.

I scan the map on my phone. "Let's try the streets near my house first," I say.

"Did she pack a bag? We should think about what was going through her head when she left," Del says.

"I didn't check," I admit.

"That's okay, we'll find her," Del says confidently.

Egan glances in the rearview mirror and frowns. "We'll try our best," he says.

* * *

Rain isn't on any of the roads near our house. She isn't in the corner shop. She isn't at the library. No one in the bus or train stations can remember seeing her. Del and I search the arcades too, checking by the slot machines and grabby hands. Then we trawl through every park in town.

After a few hours, we're out of ideas. Egan pulls into the drive-in McDonald's where he pays for three Happy Meals.

"You're going to miss orchestra," I tell him.

He sucks on his straw. "Doesn't matter," he says. His mouth is covered in mustard. I look away. I hate mustard. Even the smell of it makes me sick.

"What about the swimming pool?" Del asks from the backseat.

I shake my head and turn to him. A thick belt of sunlight is drawn across his face. His eyes are glittery and bright. Even compared to Egan Winters he's quite good looking, maybe even a bit pretty. "She doesn't have a swimsuit, I don't think."

Del smacks a hand against his head. "How could we have forgotten? The ice rink!" he says.

"Oh, Del, yes!" I say. "We have to go to the rink."

"Let me grab a McFlurry quickly," Egan says.

"We haven't got time for McFlurries," Del says bossily. I smile. He's something else, Del Holloway—something really special.

We speed up Beckett Hill, and Egan pulls the car to a shuddering halt outside the rink. Del and I hop out. Hope fizzes in me as I imagine Rain in a pair of thick blue skates, wobbling on the ice. She has to be here. It's the last possible place.

But almost as soon as I start to feel hopeful, I'm deflated again. The rink is empty. The café's not even open. No one has seen a girl that matches Rain's description.

The corners of my eyes prickle, but before I cry, Del has his arm around me. "Don't get all weepy, you. It's not helpful."

"What if . . ."

"Don't even say it, Apple."

"What if she's dead?" I splutter.

"Oh, shut up!" Del shouts and points an accusing finger at me. "If you think she's dead, we might as well go home."

I hold Jenny against me and squeeze. "What's so bad about pretending a doll's a real baby? It was weird, but Rain wasn't hurting anyone, and it made her happy," I say. I'm not sure Del can understand a word I'm saying through the choking tears.

"It made her happy?" Del looks doubtful. He pulls me toward him and wipes his arm across my face to get rid of the snot. "Apple?"

"Yeah?"

"When I met you, you were a bit of a grump, but it was like the grumpiness was an act or something. I don't think it's an act now, is it?"

A rock hits the pit of my stomach. "No," I say. The grumpiness isn't an act. Sometimes I feel like I'm full of hard music and spikes. "It doesn't matter about me. We have to find Rain."

Del takes a deep breath. "We haven't tried your nan's house," he says. He puts his hand on my shoulder. "She can't be angry. You haven't done anything wrong."

"You don't know her," I say.

*　*　*

I knock and knock and knock at Nana's door, but the only thing I manage to do is make Derry howl and sniff at the letter box. I take out my phone and dial Nana's number. It rings then goes to voice mail.

Del is at the gate. "Well?" he asks.

"She's missing too. What's *happening*?" It's like I'm in some awful dream, running after people and unable to find any of them.

"I hate to say this, but I think it's time we spoke to the police," Del says.

Egan is out of the car. He leans on Nana's wall. "I second that proposal." He opens his jacket, pulls out a packet of cigarettes, and lights up. I don't know why I'm surprised—half the seniors smoke. I just didn't think Egan was one of them. I thought he was different. Superior to everyone else.

Egan blows smoke rings into the garden, right into Nana's favorite hydrangea bush. A rush of relief swims at me: I don't think I like Egan Winters anymore. He's being really helpful and he bought us lunch, but what I'm finding out isn't all good—he's moody and smokes, and maybe worst of all, he likes mustard.

I make kissing sounds through the letter box for Derry and head down the path as Nana's neighbor, Mrs. Humphreys, sticks her head out of a top window. She's got a towel wrapped around her hair. "Apple, is that you?"

"Yes, Mrs. Humphreys. Do you know where Nana is?"

"Oh, Apple. I was just home from bowling and was

about to jump in the bath when I saw the flashing lights. The paramedics took her out on a stretcher. But I thought you were with her. Where've you been?"

"Nana's sick?"

Mrs. Humphreys throws her hands into the air. "I've no idea. As I said, all I saw was the ambulance taking her away. Oh, I hope she's all right. She told me she hasn't felt herself lately."

"Did they take her to Brampton University Hospital?" I ask.

"Well, they didn't airlift her to London, that's for sure," Mrs. Humphreys says.

Del is behind me. He takes my hand and pulls me down the path.

"What's wrong now?" Egan asks.

"Change of plan," I tell him. "We have to go to the hospital."

poetry

44

I'm out of the car door before Egan has come to a complete stop. Del calls something after me. I don't hear what it is because I'm already through the automatic doors and in the emergency waiting room. It's full of blood-smeared children and gloomy adults gripping white plastic cups. I can't see Nana anywhere.

I go to reception. "I'm looking for Bernadette Kelly," I say.

A woman with orange hair and a faint mustache yawns.

I slap my hands against the desk. "I'm her granddaughter, and an ambulance brought her here. Where is she?"

The woman doesn't flinch. She types into a computer and whispers something to her colleague. Why the whispering? My heart shrinks. My head thrums. I grip the desk.

The woman checks her computer screen again. She covers her mouth with her hand, and I get ready for the bad news. I wait to hear what I never really thought I'd have to hear because I thought Nana would live forever. I thought she'd somehow manage to outwit God.

"Mrs. Kelly is in Ward B. But she's waiting to see a doctor. You can't go down there."

Everything around me disappears. Nana's in a ward and waiting for a doctor. That means she can't be dead. She's alive. Nana's alive. I ignore the woman at the desk, scan the signs for Ward B, and run. I run so fast I almost trip over a wheelchair parked in the corridor.

"Nana!" I shout as I reach the ward and scamper through it.

A nurse frowns and puts a finger to her lips. "Shh."

"NANA!" I shout again.

In a panic I throw back curtain after curtain. Families huddled around beds frown and grumble.

Then I feel a hand tug at my arm. "Stop that," a young nurse says.

"Please help me find my grandmother." I start to cry.

The nurse puts her arm around me. "Is her name Bernadette?" she asks.

"Yes, yes, that's her."

"Come with me." She doesn't tell me not to worry. She doesn't try to reassure me. She takes me to the other end of the ward and pulls back a curtain.

Nana is lying with her eyes closed.

"Nana!" I exclaim.

"You'd be best to let her sleep," the nurse says.

But I can't. I throw myself at her even though her foot is raised and she has a bloody bandage wrapped around her head.

"Apple? Oh, Apple!" Nana's eyes open and she rubs them. Tears form at the corners.

"I was so worried. I thought . . ." I squeeze my eyes shut.

"I'll leave you to it then," the young nurse says and disappears.

I sit silently staring at Nana's ankle. I have such a big apology sloshing around in my head, but every time I open my mouth to speak, I hesitate—it doesn't feel like the time or place for it, and I'm not even sure where to begin.

"What happened?" I ask.

Nana laughs. "I'm a stupid old thing. Went into the garden to hang out the washing and didn't I turn right over on my ankle. Fell down the steps and knocked my foot and my head."

I sit in the chair next to her bed as a doctor with a too-big coat appears. She taps one of Nana's toes with a pencil. "The ankle's severely sprained but luckily there's no break. We'll keep you here a few hours to monitor the head injury, which seems superficial, and then you can go," she says. She talks directly to Nana's toe.

"But I've defrosted a piece of pork for lunch," Nana says.

"Afraid you won't be doing much cooking for a while, Mrs. Kelly, or standing on your feet at all. Do you live with someone who can help you get around?"

Nana tuts. "I'll be absolutely grand on my own."

The doctor sighs impatiently. She finally looks at Nana. "What about a neighbor?"

"Mrs. Humphreys? I hardly know her. And I wouldn't want her poking through my cupboards."

I put a hand on Nana's arm. "I'll help," I say.

"Great," the doctor says unenthusiastically. "I'll send in a nurse with the support boot and crutches to show you how you'll hobble around for the next few weeks. Remember—keep the weight off it. We don't want to see you again."

Without another word, the doctor marches away, scanning a list on her clipboard as she goes.

"Well, she has a charming bedside manner," Nana says.

I giggle and pull my chair closer to Nana's bed.

"I'll be fine taking a taxi home," Nana says. "You should call your mother and get her to pick you up."

"I'm not leaving you," I say.

Nana suddenly frowns. She's looking at a clock on the wall. "Shouldn't you be at school?"

"School doesn't matter. You're sick."

Nana shakes her head. That isn't what she means. "How did you know I'd fallen?"

I tense. I was planning to tell Nana everything anyway, but now it's come to it, I don't know where to begin. So I tell her the most important bit. "Rain's missing. Nana, I didn't know what to do. I came to your house to tell you. Mrs. Humphreys saw me and said you'd been carted off in an ambulance."

"Rain's missing? Has Annie told the police?"

"No," I mutter.

"Why did Rain run away? Is Annie out looking for her?"

I bite my bottom lip. "Nana, I don't know where Mum

is either. She went to London on Sunday and hasn't come home. It's been two nights. She doesn't even know Rain's missing."

"What do you mean two nights?" Nana sits up in bed and winces. "Why didn't you tell me straightaway? And why didn't you stay with me? Am I that bad? Have I treated you *that* badly?"

"No!" I protest. "I don't know what I was thinking. I wasn't thinking." I pick at a small scab on my hand.

"Is there anything else I should know?" Nana asks.

I shake my head. There's a lot I've left out; it doesn't mean Nana has to know what it is. Not now anyway.

"The thing is to find Rain. We'll speak to the police. *I'll* speak to them." Nana presses the call bell then uses her fingers to make the sign of the cross on her forehead, chest, and two shoulders. She closes her eyes and mumbles a prayer under her breath.

My phone beeps, and Nana opens one eye. My body tightens and I check the messages. But it isn't Rain. It's Del. Is ur nan OK????

I type back a quick message: Shes OK. I have to stay with her. Can u find Rain? Pleeease.

I'll find her, Del replies, and I believe he will.

He has to.

45

Three hours later, Nana gets discharged. We order a cab to take us home. On the way, Mum finally calls. I should be elated. I haven't even got the energy to feel relieved. I look at her name lighting up my phone, and wait a few rings before answering.

"Oh, Apple, what's going on? I'm on a train and I got your messages. Is everything okay? Apple?"

"Rain's missing, Mum," I tell her.

She doesn't answer.

Nana snatches the phone from me and yells into it. "Where the hell are you, Annie? On a train? A train to *where*? I don't know how you can call yourself a mother. Rain's been missing since last night, and you've only found out a day later. Just so you know, if anything's happened to that child, I'll make sure you pay for it. Do you hear me? Annie? Annie?"

Nana stares at the phone. "She cut me off," she says.

"Is she on her way back?"

"Who knows," Nana says.

* * *

I help Nana into her favorite chair, not that it's easy with Derry jumping all over us, and go to the kitchen to put on the kettle. Making tea seems like such a shallow thing to do with Rain still missing, but I'm out of ideas. We've filed a missing person's report with the police, and they have alerted all of their squad cars in the area. They'll wait until eight o'clock tonight to start an official search.

I already feel in my heart that it's too late.

The kettle gurgles, and my phone beeps.

It's Del again. **Where r u? Egan's bro needs the car. He's dropping me home but I'll search by foot once I've told Mum where I am. OK?????**

I'll be at urs in 10 mins, I text back.

I make Nana a mug of tea and some toast with thick-cut marmalade. "I'm going out to look for Rain again," I tell her.

Nana blows into her mug. "No, Apple. I don't want you getting lost too." She reaches for the phone. "I've remembered that Patricia Barnet's son is an inspector over in Southend. I'll see if he can pull a few strings with some friends at the station here."

"Nana, I have to find Rain," I say quietly.

"I already told you—" she begins.

I interrupt. "I know what you told me, Nana. But I'm not a baby anymore, and if we're going to be friends again, you have to start trusting me."

"After this? How can I, Apple?" The clock on the mantelpiece chimes. It's six o'clock—twenty-two hours since I last saw Rain.

"I never tried to lie. I was protecting Mum. I knew what you'd think if I told you she went to London and left us," I say.

"Everyone has been so irresponsible, Apple. You and your mother."

"I know, Nana." I put my phone into my pocket. I kiss Derry on the nose. Then I head for the hall. Jenny is lying at the bottom of the stairs. I strap her against me.

"Apple!" Nana shouts. She can't come after me with her sprained ankle; she can only shout and be disappointed.

"I'll be back soon. I'm on the phone if you need me." I

pause as I open the front door. The street lamps are flickering pink. "I love you," I say. And I'm gone.

*   *   *

Del is sitting on his front wall swinging his legs. "We searched everywhere," he says.

"I know you did," I tell him. I sit next to him, and he pats the top of Jenny's head. He looks tired and much sadder than I've ever seen him. "What do you think's happened to her?" I ask.

He takes my hand. "We should retrace our steps one last time. Look more carefully. Anyway, she won't have stayed in the same place all day."

"We could try the arcades again," I suggest.

"Exactly," he says. He hops off the wall but keeps hold of my hand. A few days ago I would have pulled away. But I don't today.

*   *   *

We weave in and out of the crowds at the arcades. Everywhere we go it's blank stares or definite nos. A man in a gray jacket smiles when he sees Rain's picture on my phone. "Pretty little thing, isn't she?" he says.

My insides curl up. "What's that supposed to mean?"

"Come on," Del says. He drags me away.

"What if he kidnapped her?" I shout. I point at the man who is now smirking at me like he knows something I don't.

It's after seven o'clock. Less than an hour until the police search party is sent hunting for Rain. I press my nose into Jenny's head and breathe in her smell, which is Rain's smell too.

Back on the promenade, Del squeezes my hand. "This isn't your fault, Apple," he says. I stare at him. I wish I could forget what's happening. I wish I could just disappear. I'm so sad I feel like my heart is a flower whose petals are gently falling away.

Del lets go of my hand and points at me. "Did you hear what I said?"

"Yes, I heard you," I say. I already feel like I'm drifting off somewhere else.

"You don't believe me. But it really isn't your fault. What could you have done?"

"I just wish . . . I wish I'd been nicer, that's all."

Del laughs into the sky. "That isn't really your style."

"But I knew she was upset. I mean, there was this one morning that we came down to the beach and she tried to wade in. The waves would have swallowed her up if Jenny

315

hadn't been tied to her." I pause. Del is staring at me. Why didn't I think of this earlier? It was the most obvious place. "You don't think . . ."

Del shakes his head. Shakes away the idea. "We checked the beaches. All of them. She'd have washed up. She'd . . ." He isn't convinced. He looks terrified.

"I have to go," I say and hurtle along the promenade. Del is shouting something behind me, and then he's level with me, and we are running together as fast as we can in one last-ditch effort to find Rain. Dead or alive.

* * *

The moon is reflected in the ocean like a giant white plate. If you had to choose a place to be kissed, or a place to die, this would be it.

I squint, checking along the shore for a figure, and when I see one, narrow and disappearing into the distance, I almost don't believe my eyes. I point. Del nods.

"Maybe," he says. "You go."

I run awkwardly along the soft sand toward the figure. The closer I get, the less convinced I am that it's Rain. Adults can resemble children from a distance. But then I am on her, and when she turns, her thin face drawn and

316

tired, I can't do anything except fall on my knees in front of her and cry.

"Apple?" Small fingers comb my hair.

"Rain, it's you," I say. I stand and wrap my arms around her, squeezing her so tight I almost take Jenny's head off. I kiss the top of her head—her chaotic red curls.

"I was about to come home. I did earlier, but you weren't there. I thought you'd gone to school," she says.

"School? I was looking for you all day. Didn't you see my note?"

"What note?"

"Rain, the police are about to start their official search any minute. I thought something awful had happened." But it hasn't. Rain is safe. My little sister, who I realize I love more than I even knew I could, is safe.

"I'm sorry," she says.

"No, Rain, I'm sorry. I shouldn't have said what I said about Jenny or hurt her like I did. It was cruel."

Rain stares at Jenny, and gently, I take the doll from the carrier and hand her over. Rain takes Jenny from me and kisses her.

"Thank you for taking care of her for me. But I don't think she's real, is she?" she says.

"It doesn't matter what I think. It only matters that you're happy."

"I'm not," Rain says. "I'm really not."

The waves break, and the surf tips the toes of my sneakers. "No," I say. "Neither am I."

"And I'm hungry," she says. She grins. And I do too. Because I have my sister back.

And she's hungry.

46

Before I manage to get my key into the lock, Nana opens the front door. She is leaning on her crutches. When she sees Rain, she gasps. "Thank the Lord," she says. She crosses herself and prays at the ceiling for several seconds. "Go on into the kitchen. I'll call the station and tell the police we've found her," she says. Then she turns away and hobbles into the sitting room. I think she doesn't want anyone to witness her crying.

Del and Rain sit on kitchen chairs. I open Nana's fridge. It's full of vegetables and eggs and meat wrapped in waxy paper. "What would madam like to eat?" I ask Rain.

She rubs her tummy. "A roast dinner, please."

"A roast? Seriously?" I peer into the fridge again. "Well, I suppose I could try." I finger a joint of uncooked pork.

"If you're having a roast, I'll stay for dinner," Del says.

"Of course." Nana hops into the kitchen and falls into a chair. "Give me over the bag of spuds and I'll peel them."

"I'll do the other veggies," Del says.

"What can I do?" Rain asks.

I plop the potatoes in front of Nana. "Help Nana with these," I tell Rain. I hand her a peeler. Nana gets a sharp knife for the job, which she always uses anyway, and I start on the meat, Nana giving directions from the chair.

And together we cook a roast.

*　*　*

"That was the best dinner I've had since I was at the Ritz," Del says, putting the last brussels sprout into his mouth.

"What's for dessert?" Rain wants to know.

"Well, I've ice cream in the freezer or we could have caramelized apples," Nana says.

"Both?" Rain asks.

Nana points to the fruit bowl by the stove. "Pass us a few Granny Smiths," she says.

And we have caramelized apples with chocolate ice cream.

My favorite.

*　　*　　*

When it's almost time for bed, I walk Del to the break in the fence between our gardens. We slide through to his side and sit on a log.

"Thank you," I say.

He holds my hand and shifts closer so our legs are touching. "Are you going to move back in with your nan?"

I shrug. "I don't know. Probably. If she lets me."

"She'll let you . . . And then I can use my binoculars to spy on you. Maybe I'll see your bum."

"That's a bit dodgy," I say.

"Yeah. You know I saw Mrs. Humphreys without any knickers on? I almost fainted."

"No! Ew! When?"

"A couple of weeks ago. Worst bit about it was that I didn't notice for ages because she was wearing a blouse and watching TV and then suddenly I looked down and . . ." He slaps his hands against his cheeks and screams.

I laugh. "If I move back in with Nana, you have to give me your binoculars."

"Listen, Apple, if you want to see me without my knickers on, you only have to ask."

I laugh again and so does Del, and then we're gazing at each other quietly and sort of intensely and before either of us can say or do anything to spoil it, I lean forward and kiss him.

At first it's a gentle lip kiss. But the pecking gets longer. Our lips part, and I taste the mints Nana left on the table after dinner, which Del couldn't resist. I close my eyes and Del's fingers are in my hair and my fingers are creeping beneath his coat. Our breathing gets shorter. My heart pummels my ribs.

And then Nana's voice calls out. "Apple. Apple?"

It's hard to stop kissing, but we manage to pull ourselves apart. We smile shyly.

"Talk about timing," Del says.

"She worries," I say.

"Well, you should go then." He kisses me quickly. "Just try not to think of my hot body all night or you'll never sleep."

"I'll try," I say, and crawl back through to my own garden.

I gaze at the sky. The moon is still a gleaming white dish and the stars twinkle.

I smile. Everything looks exactly as it should.

* * *

By the time I make it inside, Rain is upstairs in Nana's bed with Jenny. Nana is trying to make herself comfortable on the couch.

"You can wake me up if you need to pee in the night. I can help you up the stairs," I tell her.

"Not at all," Nana says, turning off the TV. "But if you could run up like a good girl and get me a nightie and the Bible from my bedside cabinet, I'll be grand. Your room is exactly as you left it, except I tidied up your desk a bit."

"Thanks, Nana," I say. I perch on the edge of the couch.

"Mum never showed up," I say.

"I was about to tell you that she called when you were in the garden to see if we'd found Rain. She's back at the flat. I told her not to come over, that we didn't need her here now. We'll see her in the morning." Nana's voice is hard and unforgiving. "And your father called too. He wants to come over at the weekend. I told him to call your cell phone."

"Okay," I say.

Nana smiles.

"Nana . . . why do you hate Mum so much? I mean, she's your daughter. Didn't you miss her when she was away?"

Nana studies her wrinkled hands. "Of course I did."

"She says you threw her out."

"I was always strict with her, and she hated me for it. I didn't want her smoking or drinking around you, but she was young and she couldn't live with my rules. I didn't throw her out though. She had to go. She had to escape."

"Why? Was I that bad?"

Nana pats my knee. "Annie was very sad when she left. She wasn't thinking clearly. But I thought she'd come back. She promised she would. Then year after year went by and no sign of her. It broke my heart not to see my own child. And it broke my heart to see you pine for her."

"But she kept her promise. She came back. You never gave her a chance."

Nana nods. "I suppose I was . . . jealous. Annie gave you to me to mind and then when she got bored with her high life, she snatched you away again. I thought you were mine, but you aren't. You're *her* daughter, and I shouldn't have forgotten that."

I sigh. "Why do I have to be anyone's? Can't I belong to myself?"

Nana rubs my cheek with her dry fingers. "You've grown up, Apple. When did that happen?"

"Does that mean you'll trust me to walk to school on my own?"

"You're moving back in?" Nana's face is like Christmas lights that have been switched on after a whole year in a box.

"I think Mum needs some time to focus on her acting, so I could come back for a while," I say.

"Whatever you want, Apple," Nana says.

I throw my arms around her and hug her so tight, I ache.

47

Mum shows up at seven thirty with my uniform in a carrier bag and a bunch of orange roses for Nana.

"I know a sorry won't fix anything, but for what it's worth, I am sorry, Apple," she says. Her face is drained of color.

"I thought you were dead. And then I thought Rain was dead. And then I thought Nana was dead. It's been a crappy few days," I say.

"I'm sorry," Mum says again.

I lead her into the kitchen. Nana is making breakfast even though she should be resting. Sausages and bacon wheeze and burp in the pan.

"Hello, Annie," Nana says.

"I've made an appointment with a doctor for later this afternoon to have Rain checked over and also to talk to her about the doll," Mum says.

"You say more than your prayers, Annie Kelly," Nana says, which means she doesn't believe her.

"Did you get a part in the film?" I ask Mum.

"No, I didn't." Mum puts down the flowers and the bag carrying my uniform and leans against the sideboard. "I want to be a better mother," she says.

Nana sits on a kitchen chair. "Apple, could you give us a minute?" she asks.

I know the drill. I go upstairs and Derry trails after me. We dive underneath the covers and I close my eyes, expecting to hear shouts and roars and maybe a pan being thrown, but it's silent. I can only hear Derry snuffling.

"Maybe they're making up, making up, never ever, ever breaking up," I say aloud.

"What are you talking about?" It's Rain.

I throw back the covers and edge over in the bed. Rain climbs in. When she feels Derry writhing at her feet, she squeals.

"Silly dog," she says.

"Where's Jenny?" I ask.

Rain ruffles Derry's hair. "She's in bed. She doesn't need me all the time."

"Really?" I ask hesitantly.

Rain shakes her head. "I don't think so. Do you?"

I smile. "No," I say. Maybe she isn't able to let go of Jenny yet, but it's a start.

Rain lies back in the bed, and Derry licks her face until she squawks. She pulls the covers over her head. "Is Mom downstairs?" she asks, her voice muffled.

"Yeah. I think her and Nana are having a serious talk."

"What are they saying?"

"I don't know. Let's invent something. I'll be Nana."

Nana/Me: Where have you been the last two days?

Mum/Rain: I was at Buckingham Palace. The queen threatened to chop off my head if I left.

Nana/Me: Doesn't Her Majesty have a phone?

Mum/Rain: She kept me chained up in a dark tower.

Nana/Me: Oh, Annie, that's awful. Come here and let me give you a hug.

Mum/Rain: I'm sorry I got everybody so worried.

Nana/Me: And I'm sorry I thought the worst. Do you want some tea?

Mum/Rain: Have you got any wine?

We giggle.

"You should go down and see Mum," I say.

Rain puts her arms around my waist. "I want to live wherever you're living," she says.

Before I can respond, someone is knocking on my

door. Derry barks, then Mum appears. She looks even sadder than she did when she arrived.

"Hi, girls," Mum says.

She sits on the bed. She takes one of my hands and one of Rain's. "I think a family meeting is overdue." She squeezes my hand. "Would you give me a *second* second chance, Apple?"

"Can I think about it?" I ask. It's too soon after everything to know what to do for the best.

"Of course," Mum says. She inches closer to Rain. "And what about you? Will you forgive me?"

"What for?" Rain replies.

"For everything, Rain."

I scoot out of the room. Before I showed up, it was just Mum and Rain, like it had always been Nana and me, and maybe it's okay for it to be like that again sometimes.

Nana is piling fried food onto four plates. I make her sit down, and I finish scrambling the eggs, then set the table and dish baked beans and mushrooms onto the plates. It smells delicious. Without waiting for Mum or Rain to come down, I dive in. It's the first hot breakfast I've had in weeks. It tastes so good.

"Nana, what's going to happen with Rain? Can she live here?" I ask.

Nana nods. "I've offered for both Annie and Rain to stay here until Annie finds her feet. She said she'll think about it."

"She's not going back to America?" I ask. It was my biggest fear. That I would betray Mum and lose her again. But lose her forever.

"I don't think she wants to go anywhere at the moment. I think we're all going to take a break from making decisions for now," Nana says.

My phone beeps: Walk to school with me? I'll let you touch my binoculars ;)

I smile and message Del back: Can u leave now? I have to go 2 the computer lab 2 finish off sum hmwk.

I wriggle into my uniform, call a good-bye up the stairs to Mum and Rain, and kiss Nana's cheek.

"Don't build a boat or anything while I'm at school," I tell her. "*Rest*."

"Aye, aye, captain," Nana says. "You're sure you'll be safe walking to school?"

I could roll my eyes or tut or stomp off in a rage. I don't because Nana's just trying to protect me. She doesn't want me getting kidnapped.

"I'll text you when I get there," I promise, and I skip out the door.

48

Del sits next to me in the computer room, caressing my neck and kissing my face and generally distracting me from my homework. I'm trying to get Mr. Gaydon's assignment typed up before the bell rings.

For the second time, I don't bother writing a fake backup. I just write the truth, every word of it, and print it out ready to hand in.

"What have you loved?" I ask Del as we leave the computer room.

He scratches his chin. "Do you have to ask?" He flutters his eyelashes.

"You're so cheesy," I say.

He bows. "I aim to cheese." He reaches into his mermaid bag. "Actually, that reminds me. I got you something." He pulls out a small bar of Toblerone. "For you," he says.

*   *   *

Del and I walk hand in hand, heads in the air, into registration. Everyone gapes; no one even expected to see me back in school again, let alone holding hands with a boy.

Pilar and Donna are sitting at the back. Donna is admiring herself in a hand mirror and patting her nose with powder. Pilar is reading a tattered paperback. When Del and I take the desk next to them, Pilar looks up amazed and gives me a wary half smile, like she isn't sure whether she should be acknowledging my existence or not. I don't wait to see what Donna's reaction is. I don't want to know.

Mrs. Wilkins takes attendance and on my way out asks to see me. "You're back again, Apple," she says, haphazardly stacking a pile of books under her arm.

"Yes, miss," I say.

"Well, that's good news. Doctor Dillon was under the impression we were going to have to involve . . ." Mrs. Wilkins sees Del at my side and changes her mind about whatever it was she was going to say. "Okay, get to class. We can talk another time."

On the way to English, Del and I run into Egan Winters in the corridor. He's talking loudly into his phone.

"All right, mate," Del says.

Egan sees us and hangs up. "Ugh. My brother winds me up. But that's what brothers do, I suppose."

"And sisters," I say.

"Del told me you found Rain," Egan says.

"Yeah. And my mum."

Egan nods. "I gotta run to a lesson. But I'm glad everything's worked out," he says. He hesitates then gives me a quick hug. He high-fives Del. And he rushes off.

Someone taps my shoulder. I turn. It's Donna Taylor. And Pilar.

"You're friends with *Egan Winters*?" Donna asks.

I sniff like it's no big deal. I know it is. In our school, it's a very big deal.

Donna pokes me. "So, will you introduce me to him?"

"Egan? Don't you think he's a bit weird?" Del says. Del still doesn't know what's happened between Egan and me. He wouldn't understand. And even if he did, he doesn't need to know.

"Weird?" Donna says. She smirks. "Uh, no. I think you'll find that *you're* the weirdo and Egan Winters is perfect."

"Del isn't weird," I say.

Donna laughs so loudly it seems like a kind of performance. "Isn't he?"

I was so happy to be coming back to school, I forgot about how truly nasty Donna could be. And I didn't expect her to start harassing me straightaway. Couldn't she have given me a day to settle back in? Would that have been too much to ask?

"No, he isn't weird," I repeat. My voice wobbles. I take Del's hand.

Donna laughs harder. "Anyway, Crab Apple, you and your *boyfriend* make a lovely couple," she says. She links arms with Pilar, who is staring at us.

My insides tighten. I'm not sure why Donna does this to me, but what I *do* know is that if I don't stand up to her now, I'll be putting up with her nastiness all year, maybe next year and the year after that too. So I hold my breath and take a step toward her. She quits laughing, coughs, and pulls Pilar closer.

"Got something to say?" She sneers.

"The thing is, Donna, I actually couldn't give a crap what you think because you're just a spiteful cow. So why don't you pick on someone who cares?" I say. I breathe hard and wait for Donna to slap me or to say something crushing.

But she just blinks and flicks her hair over her shoulder. "Loser," she mutters and stomps off, leaving Pilar behind.

Del laughs. "Loser? That's it? Someone give that girl a comedy award."

"It wasn't much of a comeback, was it?" I say, and laugh too, relieved. I'm not sure I've beaten Donna, but I think I've managed to swat her away for the time being.

Pilar is biting away a smile. "You've upset her," she says.

I shrug.

"You're back at school then," Pilar goes on.

"Looks like it," I say.

"That's good," she says.

"Pilar, aren't you coming?" Donna screeches from halfway down the corridor. Her face is all scrunched up.

"You'd better run along," I say.

Pilar rolls her eyes. Maybe she wants to be friends again, but she'll have to wait. And she'll have to say sorry for ditching me in the first place.

"We've got to go anyway," I say. I turn away.

Del throws his arm over my shoulder, and we march off.

In English, Mr. Gaydon stops by my desk while every-one else is working. "Nice to have you with us again," he says.

"Thank you, sir."

"I read the poems you e-mailed to me. All I can say is . . . wonderful."

"What poems?" Del asks.

"None of your beeswax, Mr. Holloway," Mr. Gaydon snaps.

Del shrugs and continues writing.

"And I wanted to give you this, Apple," Mr. Gaydon says. He hands me a flyer with the words *Poetry Competition* splattered across it in neon yellow. "Each school can submit one poem. It's a national award, and I once had a student who won a bronze medal. I'm hoping for a medal this year too. Maybe a gold. And I was also hoping you'd let me send in one of yours." Mr. Gaydon is not a shy or easily embarrassed person, but his neck is pink.

My own face flushes. Teachers never pick me for any-thing except cleaning-up duties.

"Could we choose the poem together? Or maybe I could write a new one," I say. I think things in my life will be different now. I want to write about how different they are.

Mr. Gaydon smiles. "Of course. Brilliant. Yes, Apple, you should write a brand-new one especially for the competition. I can help you edit it."

Del isn't supposed to be listening, but when Mr. Gaydon goes back to his desk, he nudges me. "Dork," he says. He isn't being mean or jealous. He is grinning because he is happy for me.

"Okay, you lot," Mr. Gaydon says. "The last poem in this unit is a portion of 'The Great Lover' by the very handsome Rupert Brooke."

Sharon Bowerman gives Mr. Gaydon a thumbs-up.

Jim Joyce wolf whistles.

"Have you all written your responses to it for homework?"

There is uniform nodding.

"Shall I read the poem aloud, sir?" Donna Taylor asks. She must have made up with Mr. Gaydon while I was away.

"That's very nice of you, Donna. But you know what, I think I'll do it," Mr. Gaydon says. He cracks his knuckles and reads. He has a voice like the ones you hear on the radio. We all stare. Even the boys.

"'The Great Lover' by Rupert Brooke,

"*These I have loved:*

White plates and cups, clean-gleaming,
Ringed with blue lines; and feathery, faery dust;
Wet roofs, beneath the lamp-light; the strong crust
Of friendly bread; and many-tasting food;
Rainbows; and the blue bitter smoke of wood;
And radiant raindrops couching in cool flowers;
And flowers themselves, that sway through sunny
    hours,
Dreaming of moths that drink them under the moon;
Then, the cool kindliness of sheets, that soon
Smooth away trouble; and the rough male kiss
Of blankets; grainy wood; live hair that is
Shining and free; blue-massing clouds; the keen
Unpassioned beauty of a great machine;
The benison of hot water; furs to touch;
The good smell of old clothes; and other such—
The comfortable smell of friendly fingers,
Hair's fragrance, and the musty reek that lingers
About dead leaves and last year's ferns . . ."

I listen until the end of the poem with my eyes closed,

picturing every one of the things that Rupert Brooke loves.

When I open my eyes, Mr. Gaydon is watching me. He smiles.

"It's a pretty moving piece, don't you think?" he says. If anyone disagrees, they don't say so.

Mr. Gaydon turns to the board and starts to write on it. "The poet Seamus Heaney wrote the poem 'Blackberry-Picking,' which you all read earlier this term," Mr. Gaydon reminds us. "And Heaney once said that he believed in this." He stops writing and stands back so we can read what's on the board:

poetry's ability—and responsibility—to say
what happens

"And that's what I hope you have all done this term in your homework. It isn't easy, but telling something as it is, telling the truth, always seems more beautiful and poetic than anything else," Mr. Gaydon says.

I think of all the lies I've written and passed off as true. I don't feel any regret about it, it was self-preservation, but it was such a waste of time.

"I'm probably hoping for a miracle," Mr. Gaydon

says, scanning the classroom, "but I don't suppose any of you would like to read out your poems? Anyone willing to tell us what they've loved over the course of their lives?"

The room is silent. It's probably the most personal thing Mr. Gaydon has ever made us write. The thought of reading it cold to the whole class is scary.

I glance at my poem. Could I risk sharing it? Do I have the courage?

I raise my hand, and everyone stares at me for the second time that day.

"Apple? You want to read your work to the group?" Mr. Gaydon asks.

"Yes," I say.

"And is what you've written true?"

"Well . . ." All eyes cling to me. "Emily Dickinson is a poet, and in one of her poems she says that when you tell the truth, you tell it slanted. So it's true. But it's not in-your-face true," I say. "Is that okay?"

Mr. Gaydon looks like a proud parent—or what I imagine a proud parent would look like.

"Please read it," he says, and I do.

"'These I Have Loved' by Apple Apostolopoulou,

"These I have loved:

    Pork with applesauce; tea in a heavy mug;
The smell of new books, and musty ones;
A girl with red coils for curls
—Her scream—Her smile;
The slap of a blond dog's tongue
Against my face; and an old face—Nana's;
A broken fence—a secret pathway between two
    houses;
The sinking into a familiar bed,
Sheets white and crispy clean;
The return of a woman in a green coat—
Imperfect and human; the sound of poetry;
And of pencil lead scuffing the page as I write;
Made-up stories; and Truth.
These I have loved."

The classroom is so silent I can hear the wall clock ticking. *Tick-tock, tick-tock.* For what feels like a full minute. I breathe through my nose, and Del holds my hand.

"Bloody hell. You got good at writing poems while you were away," Jim Joyce says loudly. He doesn't follow this up with a joke. He just gazes at me. And so does everyone else.

"Thanks, Jim," I say.

Mr. Gaydon raises his arms. "It's like I told you all: poetry is transforming," he says. "Right, Apple?"

"Yep," I say, and slip the poem between the pages of my special gray exercise book.

I have been transformed.

acknowledgments

Special gratitude is due to Julia Churchill, Ele Fountain, Emma Bradshaw, Helen Vick, and Ani Luca. Thank you also to everyone in the teams at Bloomsbury, RepForce Ireland, and Combined Media.

Finally, thank you and much love to my family and friends for their continued patience and support.

ANDREAS MICHALITSIANOS

SARAH CROSSAN grew up in Dublin and London, where she spent most of her time writing poems and stories and making her own books. Later, at university, she studied philosophy, literature, and creative writing. She has also taught English in the United States, and now writes full time in Hertfordshire, England, where she lives with her family. She is the author of the acclaimed *The Weight of Water*, which was shortlisted for the Carnegie Medal; *One*, which was the winner of the Carnegie Medal and the YA Book Prize in the United Kingdom; and the novels *Breathe* and *Resist*.

www.sarahcrossan.com
@SarahCrossan